Panda Books

Lilies and Other Stories

Ru Zhijuan was born in Shanghai in 1925. In 1943 she joined a theatrical group entertaining troops of the New Fourth Army. She published her first short story in 1950 and in 1955 joined the Chinese Writers' Association and the editorial staff of *Literary Monthly*.

Many of the themes of her early stories were drawn from the War of Liberation, but she now writes on a wide range of subjects. "A Badly Edited Story" won a 1979 national best short story award. Her works are well constructed with a strong emphasis on subtle characterization.

Ru Zhijuan

Lilies
and Other Stories

Panda Books

Panda Books
First edition 1985
Copyright 1985 by CHINESE LITERATURE
ISBN 0-8351-1332-9

Published by CHINESE LITERATURE, Beijing (37), China
Distributed by China International Book Trading Corporation
(GUOJI SHUDIAN), P.O. Box 399, Beijing, China
Printed in the People's Republic of China

CONTENTS

Lilies

MID-autumn, 1946.

When our coastal command decided to launch a general offensive against the Kuomintang forces, some of us in the concert group were sent by the commander of the leading regiment to lend a hand in different combat companies. Probably because I was a woman, the commander kept me till one of the very last before finally assigning me to a first-aid post near the front. I put on my rucksack and followed the messenger sent to show me the way.

It had rained that morning, and though the weather had cleared the road was still slippery, and the crops on either side sparkled fresh and green in the sunlight. There was a moist freshness in the air. If not for the sporadic booming of the enemy artillery which was firing at random, you could have imagined you were on your way to a fair.

The messenger strode along in front of me. Straight off, he put a distance of about a dozen yards between us. Because my feet were blistered and the road was slippery, try as I might I could not catch up with him. If I called to him to wait, he might think me a coward; but I couldn't hope to find the post alone. He began to annoy me.

The funny thing was that he seemed to have eyes in the back of his head, for presently he stopped of his own accord. He didn't look at me, though, just stared ahead. When I had nearly struggled up to him, he strode off again, promptly leaving me a dozen yards behind. Too exhausted to catch up, I plodded slowly along. But it was all right. He neither let me fall too far behind nor get too close to him, keeping at a distance of a dozen yards. When I quickened my step, he swung along with big strides; when I slowed down, he started sauntering too. Oddly enough, I never caught him looking back at me. I began to feel curious about this messenger.

I had barely glanced at him at regimental headquarters. Now I saw he was a tall young fellow, but pretty strong judging by his strapping shoulders. He was wearing a faded yellow uniform and puttees. The twigs in the barrel of his rifle seemed put there more for ornament than camouflage.

Though I couldn't overtake him, my feet were swollen and smarting. I called out, suggesting that we stop to rest, and sat down on a boundary stone. He sat on another stone further on, his gun across his knees and his back to me, ignoring my existence completely. I knew from experience that this was because I was a girl. Girls always had trouble like this with bashful young fellows. Feeling rather disgruntled, I went over and sat down defiantly opposite him. With his young, ingenuous round face, he looked no more than eighteen at the most. My closeness flustered him. He didn't know what to do. He hardly liked to turn his back on me, but it embarrassed him to look at me and he couldn't very well get up either. Trying hard to keep a straight face, I asked where he was from. Flushing up to his ears, he cleared his throat and told me:

"Tianmushan."

So we were from the same district!

"What did you do at home?"

"Helped haul bamboo."

I glanced at his broad shoulders, and through my mind flashed a picture of a sea of vivid green bamboo, with a narrow stone path winding up and up. A broad-shouldered lad with a square of blue cloth over his shoulders was hauling young bamboos whose long tips rattled on the stones behind. . . . That was a familiar sight in my home village. At once I felt drawn to my young fellow countryman.

"How old are you?" I asked.

"Nineteen."

"When did you join the army?"

"Last year."

"Why did you join?" I couldn't help asking the questions, though I realized this sounded more like a cross-examination than a conversation.

"When the army passed through my village, I came along with it."

"What family do you have?"

"Mum, dad, a younger brother and sisters, an aunt who lives with us."

"Are you married?"

". . . ." He flushed and fumbled with his belt, looking more sheepish than ever. With his eyes on the ground, he laughed awkwardly and briskly shook his head. It was on the tip of my tongue to ask if he had a fiancée, but I bit the question back.

After we had sat there, tongue-tied, for a while, he looked at the sky and then at me, as if to say: "Time to move on!"

It was two in the afternoon by the time we reached

the first-aid post. This was set up in a primary school three *li* from the front. Six buildings of different sizes were grouped roughly in a triangular formation, and the weeds in the yard between showed that classes has stopped for some time. We arrived to find several orderlies there preparing dressings, and the rooms filled with doors taken off their hinges and laid across bricks to serve as beds.

Presently a cadre from the local government came in, his eyes bloodshot from working late at night. To shade his eyes from the light, he had stuck a cardboard visor under his old felt hat. He had a gun over one shoulder, a scale over the other, and was carrying a basket of eggs and a large pan. He walked in, panting, put down these things, and between sips of water and bites at a ball of cooked rice produced from his pocket apologized for the state things were in. I was so fascinated by the speed with which he did all this that I hardly heard what he was saying, simply catching something about bedding which we would have to borrow. I found out from the orderlies that as the army quilts had not arrived but casualties who had lost blood were extremely susceptible to the cold, we had better borrow quilts from the villagers. Just one or two dozen mattresses would be better than nothing. Anxious to be of some use, I volunteered for the job, and because it was urgent asked my young fellow countryman to help me before he left. After a second's hesitation he agreed.

We went to a nearby village, where he turned east, I west. Before long I had handed out three receipts for two mattresses and one quilt. Heavily laden as I was, my heart was light, and I had decided to deliver these and come back for more when the messenger walked over — empty-handed.

"What happened?" The people here were so solidly behind our army and so hospitable that I couldn't understand why they had refused to lend him bedding.

"You go and ask them, sister. . . . These feudal-minded women!"

"Which house? Take me there." He must have said the wrong thing and annoyed someone. Getting one quilt less didn't matter, but offending the local people would have serious consequences. He stood there as if nailed to the ground till I reminded him quietly how important it was not to offend the masses and what a bad effect this was likely to have. At once he led the way.

No one was stirring in the hall of the house we entered. A blue curtain with a red border on top hung over the door of the inner room, and on both sides were pasted in bright red characters: "Happiness". Standing there, I called several times: but no one answered though we heard movements inside. Presently the curtain was raised and a young woman appeared. She was very pretty with fine features, arched eyebrows and a fluffy fringe. Her clothes were homespun, but new. Since she had done her hair like a married woman, I addressed her as elder sister-in-law, apologizing if the messenger had said anything to annoy her. She listened with a slightly averted face, biting her lips and smiling. When I had finished, she simply hung her head and went on biting her lips as if to keep from laughing. I scarcely knew how to bring out my request. But the messenger was watching me intently, as if I were a company commander about to demonstrate some new drill. Putting on a bold front, I asked bluntly for a quilt, explaining that our soldiers were fighting for the common folk. She listened to this without smiling, glancing from time to time back into her room. Then she looked first at me and next at the messenger, as if to weigh my words. The next moment she went in to fetch a quilt.

The messenger seized this chance to protest:

"Well, I never! I told her the same thing just now, but she wouldn't listen."

I threw him a warning glance, but it was too late. She was already at the door with the quilt. At last I understood why she hadn't wanted to lend it. It was a flowered quilt, completely new. The cover was of imitation brocade, with countless white lilies on a rich red ground. As if to provoke the messenger, she held the quilt out to me, saying:

"Here you are!"

Since my hands were full, I nodded to the lad. He pretended not to see. When I called him he pulled a long face, and with downcast eyes took the bedding and turned to rush off. There was a ripping sound — his jacket had caught on the door and torn at the shoulder. Quite a large rent it was. With a smile, the young woman went in to fetch needle and thread, but he wouldn't hear of her mending it. He went off with the quilt.

We hadn't gone far when someone told us that the young woman was a bride of three days' standing, and this quilt was all the dowry she had. That upset me, and the messenger looked unhappy too as he stared in silence at the quilt in his arms. He must have felt as I did, for he muttered to me as we walked:

"How could we know we were borrowing her wedding quilt? It's too bad. . . ."

To tease him, I said solemnly: "Yes. To buy a quilt like this, ever since she was a girl she must have got up at dawn and gone to bed late, doing all sorts of extra jobs to make a little money. Think how much sleep she may have lost over it! Yet I heard someone call her feudal-minded. . . ."

He halted suddenly.

"Well — let's take it back!"

"You'd only hurt her feelings, now that she's lent it." I was amused and touched by the earnest, unhappy look on his face. There was something extraordinarily lovable about this simple young countryman of mine.

He thought that over and evidently decided I was right, for he answered:

"All right. Let it go. We'll wash it well when we've done with it." Having settled this in his mind, he took all the quilts I was carrying, slung them over his shoulders and strode quickly off.

Back at the first-aid post, I told him to rejoin regimental headquarters. He brightened up immediately, saluted me and ran off. After a few steps he remembered something, and fumbled in his satchel for two buns. He held these up for me to see, after which he put them on a stone by the road, calling:

"Dinner's served!" Then he flew off. As I walked over to pick up the two stale buns, I noticed that a wild chrysanthemum had appeared in his rifle barrel to sway with the other twigs behind his ear.

He was some distance now, but I could still see his torn jacket flapping in the wind. I was very sorry I hadn't mended it for him. Now his shoulder would be bare all evening at least.

There were not many of us in the first-aid post. The man from the local government found some village women to help us draw water, cook and do odd jobs. Among them was the bride, still smiling with closed lips. She glanced at me from time to time, and kept looking round as if in search of someone. At last she asked:

"Where has that comrade gone?"

When I told her he had gone to the front, she smiled shyly and said, "Just now when he came to borrow bedding, I treated him rather badly." Then smiling she set to work, neatly spreading the mattresses and quilts we had borrowed on the improvised beds made of door-boards and tables (two tables put together is one bed). She put her own quilt on a door-board under one corner of the eaves outside.

In the evening a full moon rose. Our offensive still hadn't started. As usual the enemy was so afraid of the dark that they lit a host of fires and started bombarding at random, while the flares that went up one after the other to hang like paraffin lamps beneath the moon made everything below as bright as day. To attack under these conditions would be very hard and would surely entail heavy losses. I resented even that round, silver moon.

The man from the local government brought us food and some home-made moon cakes. Apparently it was the Moon Festival!

That made me think of home. At home now, for the festival, there'd be a small bamboo table outside each gate, with incense and candles burning beside a few dishes of sunflower seeds, fruit and moon cakes. The children would be waiting impatiently for the incense to burn out so that they could share the good things prepared for the goddess of the moon. Skipping round the table, they would sing: "The moon is so bright; we beat gongs and buy sweets. . . ." or "Mother moon, please shine on me. . . ." My thoughts flew to the lad from Tianmushan who had hauled bamboos. A few years ago he had probably sung the same songs. . . . I tasted a delicious home-made cake, and imagined the messenger lying in a dugout, or perhaps at regimental headquarters, or walking through the winding communication trenches. . . .

Soon after that our guns roared out and red tracer bullets shot across the sky. The offensive had begun. Before long, casualties started trickling in, and the atmosphere grew tense in the first-aid post.

I registered the names and units of the wounded. The lighter cases could tell me who they were, but when they were heavily wounded I had to turn back their insignia or the lapels of their jackets. My heart missed a beat when under the insignia of one badly injured man I read: "Messenger". But I found he was a battalion messenger. My young friend worked in regimental headquarters. I resisted a foolish impulse to ask if casualties ever got left on the field, and what messengers did during combat apart from delivering dispatches.

For an hour or so after the offensive started, everything went swimmingly. The wounded men, as they came in, reported that we had broken through the first stockade, then the barbed wire entanglement, occupied the first fortifications, and started fighting in the streets. But at that point the news stopped. In answer to our questions, incoming casualties just told us briefly:

"They're still fighting. . . ." "Fighting in the streets." But from the mud which covered them, their utter exhaustion and the stretchers which looked as if dug out of the mire, we could imagine the fierceness of the battle.

Soon we ran out of stretchers, so that not all the heavily wounded could be sent straight to the hospital in the rear. There was nothing I could do to alleviate the men's pain, except get the village women to wash their hands and faces, give a little broth to those able to eat, or change the clothes of those who had their packs with them. In some cases we had to take off their clothes to wash away the blood and filth in which they were covered.

I was used to work like this, but the village women were shy and afraid to attempt it. They all wanted to cook instead. I had to persuade the young bride for a long time before, blushing furiously, she would consent. She only consented, though, to be my assistant.

The firing at the front was spasmodic now. I thought it must soon be dawn, but actually it was only the middle of the night. The moon was very bright and seemed higher than usual. When the next serious casualty was brought in, all the beds inside were occupied and I had him put under the eaves outside. After the stretcher-bearers laid him there, they gathered around and wouldn't go. One old fellow, taking me for a doctor, caught hold of my arm and said earnestly: "Doctor, you've got to think of a way to cure him! If you save him our stretcher-bearers' squad will give you a red flag!" The other bearers were watching me, wide-eyed, as if I had only to nod to cure the soldier. Before there was time to explain, the bride came up with water, and gave a smothered cry. I pushed through the bearers to have a look, and saw a young, round ingenuous face which had been ruddy but now was deathly pale. His eyes were peacefully closed, and the torn flap in the shoulder of his uniform was still hanging loose.

"He did it for us," said the old stretcher-bearer remorsefully. "Over ten of us were waiting in a lane to go forward, and he was just behind us when the bastards threw a hand-grenade down from a roof. The grenade was smoking and whizzing about between us. He shouted to us to drop flat, and threw himself on the thing. . . ."

The bride drew in her breath sharply. I held back my tears while I said a few words to the bearers and sent them off. When I turned back again, the bride had quietly fetched an oil lamp and undone the messenger's jacket. Gone was all her previous embarrassment, as she earnestly gave him a gentle rub down. The tall young messenger lay there without a sound. . . . I pulled myself together and raced off to find the doctor. When we got back to give him an injection, the bride was sitting at his side.

Bending over her work, stitch by stitch she was mending the tear in his uniform. The doctor made a stethoscope examination, then straightened up gravely to say: "There's nothing we can do." I stepped up and felt the lad's hand — it was icy cold. The bride seemed to have seen and heard nothing. She went on sewing neatly and skilfully. I couldn't bear to watch her.

"Don't do that!" I whispered.

She flashed me a glance of surprise, then lowered her head to go on sewing, stitch by stitch. I longed to take her away, to scatter this atmosphere of gloom, to see him sit up and laugh shyly. At that moment I felt something in my pocket — the two stale buns the messenger had given me.

The orderlies brought a coffin, and removed the quilt. The bride suddenly turned pale. Snatching up the quilt, she spread half of it on the bottom of the coffin, leaving half to cover him.

"That quilt belongs to one of the villagers," an orderly said.

"It's mine!" She turned away. Her eyes were bright with unshed tears in the moonlight. I watched as they covered the face of that ordinary country lad, who had hauled bamboo, with this red quilt dotted with white lilies — flowers of true purity of heart and love.

March 1958

Translated by Gladys Yang

On the Banks of the Cheng

NORTH, always north they streamed, along highways and byways. Troops, gun-carriages, mules, ox-carts and villagers with crates swinging from carrying poles or big packs on their backs, all headed north, leaving countless footprints in the mud as they passed. Now these depressions were brimming with rain water, but the road was deserted.

Then came a small contingent all alone. It was pressing steadily northwards at a slow pace.

This was the summer of 1947. The main force had gone swiftly ahead. These score or so of sick and wounded men plodding slowly along in the rear were headed for the time being by Zhou Yuhao, assistant company commander of the guards. They had orders to reach their objective and rejoin the main army before dusk the next day.

Zhou Yuzhao, the only experienced cadre in this group, also happened to be the one in the worst shape. Originally, he had been given the nickname of Big Bull on account of his size and strength, and he had come first in a cross-country race for men carrying full equipment. But two months of bad attacks of malaria had combined with a light head wound to reduce him to a shadow of his former self. Lending a helping hand to Young Yu of the Cultural Team, he was walking at the head of the men. Round his waist he carried hand grenades and a pistol tucked into his belt. Thin as he was, he looked a redoubtable figure. Zhou was holding Young Yu to prevent him from falling and trying not to slip himself. His heart burned as he turned to look at the men behind and realized his own weakness.

Young Yu, leaning against Zhou's shoulder, felt rather tense. He was the youngest in this group and the fittest. Apart from badly blistered feet there was nothing wrong with him. He was trying to read Zhou's face to gauge the seriousness of their situation.

They had only one day and one night to cover the 120 *li* to their destination. Zhou knew quite well what would happen if they failed to make it. They were leaving southwestern Shandong and its good people at the rate of four *li* an hour on the muddy road. Of course, they would be returning. Still, it was no joke pulling out. He was having fits of shivering, although big beads of sweat were running down his face. The malaria had hit him earlier than usual today.

Summer is a rainy season in the Shandong hills. Grey clouds hung low and heavy in the sky. There was not a breath of wind in the sultry air. The sound of approaching gunfire heightened the tension.

The pad of swift footsteps made Zhou look round and see two women overtaking them. They had probably also been left behind by their group. The elder had a large pack on her back and was clasping a wooden placard inscribed "Home of Honour".* The other, a tall young woman, well-built and with a proud bearing, held a baby in one arm while over her other shoulder

---

* A sign given to those who had a husband or son serving in the people's army.

hung a rifle from the muzzle of which dangled a bundle of pancakes. When Zhou asked where they were going, she flashed him a smile.

"The same way as you!" she replied.

"So you've given up your homes?" he said.

"What are our homes?" The elder woman smiled too. "We've got rid of everything which could be of use to the enemy. There are only a few *mu* of land. Let the enemy try to cart them away if they can!"

"The enemy won't find it any picnic on our land!" The young mother laughed. "You'll be fighting back before long. Then you must drop in on us for a cup of tea."

Still smiling, the women glided past. The pancakes tied to the rifle swayed till they caught the baby's attention, and he reached out a chubby hand to clutch at one.

The ground seemed to be heaving and burning under Zhou's feet. Once the enemy set foot here, they would surely be trapped and burned to ashes!

"Commander Zhou, I'm thirsty!" Young Yu could hardly stand the pain of his blisters, but he was not going to admit it.

"Same here! Let's put on a spurt. Once across the Cheng we'll find the going much smoother over level, sandy soil. We may even run into some villagers who'll give us a good square meal and plenty to drink. How do you fancy that?"

"Suits me!" Tears were standing in the boy's eyes. "But, company commander, you look very feverish!"

Zhou was, indeed, burning with fever. He was longing for a glimpse of that river with its cool, silver water. Even a breeze would be good! But there was not a breath of air, although black clouds were converging overhead and the sky was darkening. The moisture in the stifling air made it hard to breathe. There was going to be a storm.

A few minutes later, sure enough, a howling wind sprang up in the hills and came careering down to batter them. Planting his feet deep in the mud, Zhou raised his head to enjoy the cooling sensation of the wind on his face and chest. Hard on the heels of the wind came a flash of lightning and a great clap of thunder. Then rain started pouring down in bucketfuls.

"Take hands!" bellowed Zhou to the men behind, his own arm round Young Yu. But his voice was swallowed up by the wind and rain. It seemed as if the fury of the storm would swallow up and destroy everything on earth.

The small band plodded doggedly on through the white sheets of rain.

It was still raining and the wind was blowing hard when, towards dusk, they reached the Cheng.

The river was in spate. There was neither bridge nor ferry-boat in sight, the turbid water was eddying in whirlpools. Some of the branches and flotsam from upstream spun round these whirlpools and were sucked out of sight. Others were borne headlong downstream. The river was rising so fast that the willows on the bank were half submerged.

"Step forward, those who can swim!" shouted Zhou. "You'll help the others across."

The shouts that went up in response sounded like a declaration of war on the storm.

"I can swim too." Zhou held out a hand to Young Yu.

"No!" Young Yu backed quickly away. Zhou's out-stretched hand and his comrades' shouts had put fresh life into him. His blood was racing. "Commander Zhou," he said earnestly, "I can swim. Let me help one of the others across."

They prepared to cross. The rain had stopped as suddenly as it started, and the wind was dropping too. The water was inky black, the current was strong. Young Yu helped a man who could not swim into the river. After wading two or three steps they were out of their depth. Young Yu held his companion's head up with one hand while he struck out with the other. But almost at once the waves swamped them, the bag tied to his belt was swept away. His face white, gasping for breath as he floundered about, Young Yu yelled to the others on the bank, "It's no use! The water's still rising."

"Come back, quick!" shouted Zhou, racing along the dike to keep up with them.

Under the darkling sky, Young Yu and the other soldier climbed out, dripping. The black, swift rushing Cheng stretched like a barrier before them which no one could cross. The stars came out and the moon. The men sat down on the bank to hold an emergency meeting. The water glinting at their feet seemed to hide wild beasts which might spring out to carry them off. The sporadic rifle fire behind them was coming nearer.

They decided to send two men to find out the shallowest fording place and get some food from the local people, while the rest of them stayed on the bank and tied their puttees and pack ropes together to make an attempt at crossing. Zhou Yuzhao and Young Yu set off for the nearest village.

The village, a small one, was uncannily quiet, showing not a single light or plume of smoke. The threshing-floor had been swept clean, but there was no sign of life. As Zhou led Young Yu warily up to a hut at the entrance to the village, he saw written boldly on the mud wall the words: Beware of the Mines! He pushed open the door, which was unlatched. There was no one inside. The light of the moon showed a plank propped up in the middle of the room with another chalked inscription: "So you've come, eh? Well, you won't get away alive!"

Obviously, the whole village had evacuated.

It would be useless, not to say rash, to go on. They headed for the next village. On the way Zhou started chuckling and Young Yu followed suit, picturing the discomfiture of the enemy on their arrival here. They had neither located a ford nor found food, and enemy guns were still booming away behind them, but they felt in good heart, confident of victory.

The moon was shining fitfully through the clouds. The earth was in darkness one moment, silver the next. Crops swayed as they passed. The maize was already higher than a man and its succulent leaves were rustling. The rumble of artillery fire in the distance made the fields seem more tranquil by contrast. But a sudden sound near by alerted Zhou, who halted and held his breath. Yes, he could hear a series of thuds. Young Yu caught the sound too. Zhou was immediately on his guard, for it was hard to tell what this portended. Holding his rifle at the ready and signing to Young Yu to follow him, he tiptoed towards the sound.

The moon came out from behind the clouds, bathing everything on earth in a soft radiance. In the middle of the next field they could see a small hut, nothing else. But another thud sounded abruptly close at hand and a gruff old voice muttered, "Thirty-four."

Straining their eyes, they made out that there was a melon field just ahead, the round, glossy melons in it as big as wash-basins. And pacing through the field was a bare-headed, stooped old man, a glittering axe in his hand. He crouched down before a melon, tapped it a few times as if to see whether it was ripe, and then, having felt and stared at it for a while, slashed at it again and again with his axe and muttered, "Thirty-five." This done, he stood up and lumbered off to crouch down beside another melon and hack it to pieces.... He would not let the enemy have his melons.

Suddenly the old peasant squatted down to pick something up from the ground. For a long time he remained there motionless. Then he started sobbing quietly to himself.

"Grandad!" called Zhou Yuzhao softly, walking over. The old peasant looked up in astonishment, then rose slowly to his feet.

He was an old, old man with long white eyelashes and snowy hair. There were tears on his face. After eyeing Zhou intently for a moment, he cried in a voice that trembled:

"Comrades, is it you?"

"Yes, grandad. We. . . ." Zhou lacked the courage to complete that sentence. But the old peasant understood, for he nodded and after a pause held out his hand.

"Look at this, comrade," he said. He squatted down again to show them a damp slip of paper and a dollar note. With his other big gnarled hand he wiped his eyes.

"Two melons have gone, but this money was left under the vine." He spread the damp note carefully out on his knees. "They left money under the vine! . . . Will you read what this says, comrade?" He handed the paper to Zhou, who managed in the moonlight to decipher the faint writing. "Grandad or grandma who grew these melons, we got so thirsty marching that we've taken two and left you a dollar. Hope that's enough and that you don't mind. We were simply parched. X Company of the People's Liberation Army."

Having read this out Zhou asked, "How long ago did they pass, grandad?"

The old man looked them up and down.

"You want to cross the river?"

Zhou nodded and explained their position. The old peasant thought it over and declared:

"Never mind how high the water is. I'll see you get over tonight!" He took them into his hut, empty except for a big pack on the ground and, resting against it, a rifle and long pipe with tobacco pouch attached. Had they come any later, the old man would have been gone.

The men left by the river had not succeeded in crossing with a rope. The old melon-grower hastily called them all over, produced a basketful of sweet potatoes and lit a fire so that they could dry themselves and cook some food. This done, he disappeared.

Zhou posted a sentry and told the others to rest. After a drink of water he went out. Young Yu, lying on a heap of straw, said nothing. He felt he should go with Zhou, whose face was feverishly flushed, but his own legs seemed glued to the ground and he could not move. Sighing with mortification, he rested his head on the old man's pack and slept. Almost at once, or so it seemed, he was woken. His comrades were sprawled out sleeping, the moon was high overhead, and the rat-tat of rifle fire, which carried unusually clearly through the still night, was evidently much closer.

On the threshing-floor outside, in a patch of silver moonlight, the old man was sitting on a heap of door-boards. His face, set in serious lines, seemed carved from stone. Presently Zhou Yuzhao came back from the river with a great coil of wet rope. Stumbling with weariness, he approached the old man and said softly, "Let's try again, grandad. Make the rafts a bit smaller."

The old peasant shook his head with a frown and said sharply, "You go and have some sleep." He added more gently, "You've a long way to march once you've crossed." With that he took the ropes from Zhou and pushed him towards the hut, after which he lumbered off again.

Zhou sank down wearily beside the door. But soon he looked up at the sky and, resting his hands on the ground, raised himself with an effort to his feet.

"Commander Zhou!" Young Yu scrambled up despite himself and, stopping Zhou, said, "Let me go instead of you!"

Zhou grinned at him. "All right, we will both go and find some way out." He scanned the sky again. Orion was sinking. In another three or four hours it would be light.

"We haven't much time. We've got to cross before dawn. Otherwise we'd have to turn back." He broke off to look at Young Yu. "If we stayed here as guerrillas, lad, would you be afraid?"

"With you, I'm not afraid of anything," replied Young Yu stoutly.

Their feet brushed the dew-pearled crops by the path, frogs were croaking lustily, all around was a sea of green. Yet tomorrow this quiet loveliness. . . . Machine-guns were rattling in the distance again.

"This time tomorrow the enemy will be here." Zhou turned his head to wipe away a tear. "What you should have said, Young Yu, is this: With the people backing us, we're not afraid of anything."

Another strange sound reached them from the dike. Zhou strained his ears to listen, then hurried to the spot with Young Yu. They found the old peasant hacking away with a hoe. Going closer, Zhou saw a heap of earth beside him. The old man was cutting a ditch through the dike to the river. Stupefied for a second, Zhou suddenly understood. He grabbed hold of the hoe, protesting, "Don't do that, grandad! . . ."

The old man answered calmly, "You're just in time. Fetch the other comrades and get ready to cross."

"Grandad, we'd die sooner than harm you folk." Zhou was trembling with emotion. The old man said nothing, just eyed him narrowly.

"Where's your home, comrade?" he asked.

"North of the Yellow River."

"In the liberated area?" he asked solemnly.

"That's right."

The old man's brows contracted as he said, "Your home's liberated, that's good. Do you ever think of those places that aren't free yet? . . . I don't like the way you young fellows keep talking of dying." He snatched back the hoe, explaining reasonably, "The Cheng isn't too deep. It's just that these freshets are pouring down too fast. If I breach the dike to let some of the water out, the current will slow down and you can wade across."

"No, you can't do that!" cut in Zhou in a tone that brooked no argument. Grabbing the hoe once more, he replaced the earth.

"You stop that!" bellowed the old man furiously.

Zhou threw his arms around him, tears in his eyes.

"We're the people's army, grandad. We live for the people and we're ready to die for them."

The old peasant brandished his fist. "Talking about dying again! You sit down and listen to me." With a great sigh, he squatted down on the dike.

The firing had stopped, rather ominously it seemed. The Cheng was racing along below the dike, its glinting waves lapping the willows on the bank, whose tendrils were rippling softly in the water.

"The Cheng flows fast, everyone knows that," said the old man slowly. "I was born and bred beside it, I'm not afraid of it. In summer we boys used to jump into the river to bathe, or catch fish and play at water-battles in it. When it turned colder we caught shrimps here and dug for crabs.

"One summer there was such heavy rain that the river brimmed its banks, just like today. It was sweltering hot, but my folks wouldn't let me go swimming. One noon, when dogs' tongues were lolling out for heat and there was no wind to whip up waves on the Cheng, I slipped down on the sly for a swim, sure I had nerves and strength enough to be safe. The moment I dived in I found out my mistake. The river had become a killer! And there was no getting out. The current carried me off like a hundred powerful hands tugging at me and rushing me downstream. I was limp as a rag, weak as straw, tossed about like a cork. Soon all my strength was gone. What with all the water I'd swallowed, I was nearly done for. I had no fight left but gave myself up for lost. And then, of course, I sank. But that same instant a picture flashed through my mind. A year before, going to borrow something from my grandmother, I'd walked three or four *li* downstream and noticed an old tree growing out of the dike, shading the river and stretching one branch out over the water. It had struck me what a cool spot this would be for swimming in summer. Later the place had slipped my mind, but now I remembered that tree and it gave me hope. That hope steadied me so that my strength came back and I started fighting for my life. Somehow I managed to keep afloat till I reached that big tree and caught hold of the branch. . . . Too bad, it's withered now. What I'm trying to tell you is this: Hope isn't something you can see or grasp, yet it's mighty powerful. Without hope men can't live on, life has no meaning. Right now, you're the people's hope. So long as we have our Party and our army, even at the back of beyond we've something to fight for — we've hope. Landlords and reactionaries can rage and rampage, but we're not afraid. If there were nothing to hope for, we'd be afraid. Understand? . . ."

The Cheng was rushing and swirling at the old man's feet, pounding the banks and roaring like a savage beast.

"We understand, grandad!" In a flash, Zhou Yu-zhao had a clear vision of the future. Tomorrow this old melon-grower might be roaming the hills with his rifle; the young mother with the gun might be carrying her child through the rain; the clean, quiet village might be a mass of flames. But sooner or later the army would come back, the enemy would be wiped out, the old man would plant melons again, the baby would be taken to visit his grandmother, new homes would be built, new villages with the old names would appear. . . . Zhou looked with shining eyes from the sky dotted with stars to the river and the white-haired old man. He was taking a silent pledge that so long as a breath remained in his body he would go forward, in order to fight back later with the army. He rose, picked up the hoe and with swift, sure strokes mended the dike. Strength had flowed back miraculously into his arms. Very soon the earth was firmly tamped down in the ditch.

The old man sat there in silence and did not stop him. He stared, frowning, at the inky black water. At last he stood up, saying, "All right. Let me have a look round. You wait here. I'll be back in less time than it takes for two meals." With that he strode swiftly off.

The firing, which had stopped, started up again now more fiercely and much nearer. The men came out from the hut to the river bank.

Young Yu was sitting there as if in a trance. Ever since the day two years ago when he first put on an army uniform, he had looked on himself as a soldier. Now he suddenly realized there had been something missing.

The rain had ceased some hours ago, the water might be subsiding. Zhou Yuzhao divested himself of his hand grenades, but before he could sound the river Young Yu leapt up, tore off his cap and thrust it into Zhou's hands. The lad jumped into the river, followed by two other swimmers.

Far from subsiding, the Cheng was higher than ever, swollen by all the freshets from upstream. As the three swimmers climbed the dike again the old peasant came panting along with two middle-aged men, each with half a dozen poles over his shoulder.

"It's all right! I've caught two eels! They ran into the hills from the enemy just in time to be caught in my net!" The old man's spirits had soared and his long eyelashes were fluttering cheerfully. The two "eels" greeted the soldiers with a grin and without more ado started lashing the poles together. The old man had obviously explained what was needed and worked out the best way to cross the Cheng.

In less than the time for two meals, the old peasant had become a different man. As he worked he winked at Zhou and said:

"See, comrade, the Cheng belongs to us. However wild it is, it must obey our orders. . . . You'll get across easy, comrades. But just let the enemy try to cross, and the Cheng won't treat them so politely!" He shook with laughter.

The east was a hazy white, it would soon be dawn. The three peasants had lashed the poles together in squares. While they carried them down to the water's edge, Zhou Yuzhao divided his men into two groups, each with strong swimmers in it. Holding on to all four sides of the square, the first group entered the water.

The old man saw them off. His high spirits had given place to quiet solemnity. His lips moved for a second and he said decisively:

"I wish you a good journey, comrades! I'm too old to see you across. Don't forget our Cheng. Next year I'll be growing more melons for you to eat." He smiled and seemed on the point of saying more, but thought better of it and simply waved his hand.

The first raft was lowered on to the water and the swimmers, helped by one of the peasants, were impelling it vigorously towards the other shore. The current was so swift that soon the raft and men on it were no more than a black shape bobbing downstream. However, they contrived to inch across and gain the further side. When the second raft was lowered, Zhou Yuzhao stood in the water looking up at the old man on the dike. This second raft brought him the conviction that they were not withdrawing but advancing. On their path forward he had received a cup of cold tea from an old man's hands, the comfort of girls' pure singing, hot boiled eggs thrust into his pocket by an old village woman. . . . The old woman had left her village carrying with her the placard "Home of Honour", the young mother had taken up a gun and fastened her pancakes to it, and to frighten the enemy they had left the message: Beware of the Mines! All these things merged in his mind into one vast, invincible force personified by this indomitable old man. Stooped, but with unshakable faith, he stood there alone on the dike gazing into the distance.

The sky was grey, the river a deep blue. It rushed on bearing the people's hope, the fighters' pledges. It flowed far, far away, to water all the fields of their native land.

The small contingent marched on and on with a faith that nothing could destroy. And a stooped figure stood, motionless, on the dike.

May 1959
Translated by Gladys Yang

The Warmth of Spring

BEFORE it was light, the first tram out from the terminus rumbled past. Jinglan woke with a start, and sat up. Relieved to find it still early, she slipped out of bed. To avoid waking her husband, Mingfa, beside her, she did not put on the light but groped in the dark to pull up the quilts Dabao and Erbao had kicked off and hang up the jacket their father had dropped on a chair. Then, satisfied, she picked up her shopping basket. This was Jinglan's established custom. Every Sunday she would rise before dawn and go to market to buy Mingfa something good to eat.

"Jinglan!" She must have woken him after all. "Where are you off to so early?"

"To the market." Jinglan was not sorry he had woken. Now he could tell her what he fancied for dinner.

"What would you like to eat today?" she asked.

"Anything will do." He turned over and went back to sleep.

"Anything will do," she echoed. That's how it always was. Food? "Anything will do." Clothes? "Anything will do." Purchases for the house? "Anything will do." Yet he talked so eagerly and to the point to the other foremen in his works and even to the apprentices that Jinglan felt it wasn't fair. She kept busy from early till late, shopping, cooking and washing. During the day she sewed, and when it was too dark for sewing she used to knit. She didn't use a fan in summer, just stamped her foot if the mosquitoes bit her, not putting down her work for a minute, to make a good home for them. But all her husband said was "Anything will do", as if their home meant nothing at all to him.

Sighing softly, Jinglan left the house. The deserted road looked much broader than in the daytime. The street lamps were still on and the trees by the road cast great shadows. It was utterly still outside, except when a milkman cycled past with a rattle of milk bottles; but once the rattling faded away in the distance, all she could hear was her own footsteps padding on the pavement.

Jinglan sensed vaguely that in the last two years a barrier of some sort had grown up between her and Mingfa. Not that he lost his temper or treated her badly. On pay day he always gave her all he earned, and sometimes the two of them went to a film together. Yet Jinglan felt something was missing, though what exactly this was she couldn't say. . . .

The street lamps went out simultaneously. Day was breaking. A few stars could still be seen in the deep blue sky, while traffic and pedestrians were appearing in the street.

"I've fuel and rice at home and money in my pocket for the marketing — what more could anyone want?" Jinglan scolded herself, trying to shake off her depression.

The market was already doing a brisk business. Some stalls of fresh foodstuff were surrounded, while the vendors not yet patronized were hailing potential customers. Jinglan bought a basketful of meat and vegetables, and was on the point of starting home when she saw on a fish stall a tub of fresh-water shrimps as thick as her finger — transparent and faintly green, frisky and lively.

"What enormous shrimps!" With a lighter heart, she promptly laid out ninety-eight cents on a catty. Now Jinglan was a careful housekeeper and shrimps were not one of Mingfa's favourite dishes. It wasn't eating shrimps that was important to her, but the happy memories they conjured up for her, Mingfa and their whole family. . . .

"What enormous shrimps!"

It was the third year after Liberation. Mingfa now had a job. Their family gained a new lease of life. Jinglan brought the two boys from the country to live with their father, and they settled down to a secure existence, with no more worrying about fuel and rice. One Sunday she had brought some big, live shrimps back from the market. "Come here quick! Look at these enormous shrimps!" she called, putting them into the wash basin where they leapt about and darted this way and that. Mingfa and the children, crowding round, tickled them with straws and laughed heartily at their antics.

"Remember something, Mingfa?"

"Of course I do, Jinglan." Mingfa cast an affectionate glance at her, then hugged the two boys to him. Husband and wife were both thinking of the past.

The summer two years before Liberation, Jinglan had been living with the children in the country when Mingfa came home from town having lost his job. They had no land — how were the four of them to live? Husband and wife took it in turn to go to the river each evening to catch tiddlers and shrimps. A night's fishing generally meant a catty or so of fish and shrimps, which could be sold the next morning in the town to provide enough maize to keep the family going. One evening Jinglan had gone further than usual to fish all night at a creek downstream. As soon as it was light, she hurried joyfully home with the bamboo creel.

"Shrimps! Look at these enormous shrimps!"

And Mingfa saw big, transparent, faintly green shrimps jumping about in the creel.

"That's fine — you've got over a catty there!" His heart smote him at the sight of his wife's exhausted, jubilant face, but he tried to sound pleased.

The children were too small to share their parents' troubles. All they knew was that they were hungry and wanted to eat the big shrimps. When their father emptied the catch into a basket and set off to town to sell it, the little boys tagged after him, crying. Mingfa felt as if his heart was pierced by ten thousand fish-hooks; he looked at his sons and at his powerful hands. Why, these hands of his could fashion the finest spare parts on a lathe or cope with the hardest steel, yet here they were carrying a small basket to market, where he would set down his catch and cry his wares. His nose smarted, his heart swelled with hatred for the whole rotten social system. Roughly shaking off his sons, he strode away with moist eyes.

Bitter memories can be sweet when you are happy. So though Mingfa and Jinglan said not a word as he held the boys close and she looked with infinite content at him, both of them were sharing the same thoughts and emotions — what a wonderful splendid life they were leading now! Jinglan especially, as a wife, felt she could know no greater happiness than this.

Having bought the shrimps, Jinglan walked slowly home, turning over all these happenings in her mind. She dwelt most, though, not on the sale of shrimps before Liberation but on the purchase of shrimps after Liberation. She could remember every word, smile, glance and gesture on that occasion — she knew them all like a lesson learned by heart, and she savoured each smallest detail. When she took the shrimps home that day, Mingfa had watched her affectionately all the time till she set them fried a bright red on the table. He seemed to be saying, "We've been through thick and thin together, Jinglan, and we've won through. . . ." This recollection always made her face light up. Now, looking at the big, frisky shrimps in her basket, she smiled.

"Wool-gathering, Jinglan?" Someone caught her arm.

With a start she looked up to see plump Sister Zhu from next door, who was barring her way and greeting her loudly. Sister Zhu was chairman of the Women's Committee in their lane. A month before this, when they organized a production and welfare co-operative in the lane, she had become production chief of the team to which Jinglan belonged. She was cheery and outspoken and had once worked for two years in a textile mill. Catching hold of Jinglan, she told her earnestly, "Our team's holding a meeting this evening — a new order's come in."

"Oh!" said Jinglan.

"Are you coming or not?" demanded Sister Zhu, who had no patience with this lukewarm response.

"I'll be there." Jinglan attended most meetings, but she sat there knitting as she listened, never speaking herself. She went to hear what the others had to say, and then carried out their decisions. Sister Zhu, well aware of this weakness of hers, followed up: "Jinglan, you ought to say something at the meeting too!"

Jinglan hung her head with a shy smile. "What — me?"

There was nothing Sister Zhu could do but wag a finger at her before hurrying away.

Reaching her door, Jinglan looked at the shrimps and her heart beat faster as she wondered what Mingfa would say. He'd come over to look with a smile and the boys would press round. . . . She relived the lively scene of a few years past. Then, suppressing her excitement, she opened the door and went in. The room was very quiet. The boys, awake now, were lying on their stomachs reading in bed. Mingfa, a jacket over his shoulders, his hair sticking up in all directions because he had scratched his head so many times, was too busy at the table even to look up. The wash basin and water she had left ready for them had not been touched. The whole atmosphere was extraordinarily serious. Swallowing the words on the tip of her tongue, Jinglan quietly emptied the shrimps into a bowl which she placed in the most conspicuous position on the chest of drawers. Then she made the children wash and have their breakfast. But after they had eaten and gone out to play, Mingfa was still concentrating on whatever he was drawing and writing. Unable to contain herself any longer, she said:

"Mingfa! I bought shrimps today."

"Uh, huh."

"Look at them, aren't they enormous?" She tried to speak casually, but her voice was not quite natural.

"Uh, huh." Still he didn't look up.

"Look, Mingfa!"

At that he did raise his head to look at his wife standing self-consciously there with a bowl of shrimps in her hands.

"Bought shrimps, eh? That's fine. But you needn't have gone to so much trouble. I don't mind what I eat." He smiled at her warmly, then bent to his papers again. His smile reminded her of the way he looked at the children when he didn't want them to follow him to work. Evidently he'd not only forgotten those bitter-sweet memories — he didn't want to be disturbed by her talk.

As Jinglan slipped into the kitchen with the shrimps, her eyes filled with tears. It was early spring now, but her heart was chill. It was becoming clearer and clearer that a barrier had grown up between her and Mingfa. Not realizing that her husband's world was larger than hers, his interests wider and his aim in life higher, she wept because she felt unfairly treated.

But though her heart was in turmoil, Jinglan quietly set about dressing the shrimps, carefully clipping their whiskers one by one. Upset as she was, she cooked a good Sunday dinner, not even forgetting to heat four ounces of wine for Mingfa. She didn't forget her work team's meeting that evening either, but set off in good time with two pairs of socks which needed mending.

A month earlier, when the Production and Welfare Co-operative was set up in their lane, Jinglan had joined because everyone else was joining. For the first few days it all seemed rather strange and she would run home during the afternoon break to see if the boys were back from school and up to mischief, or whether there was any boiled water left. But later on she slipped into a new routine. She did whatever job she was given, working steadily away for eight hours, scarcely lifting her head. When the other women complimented her on working so hard, she was pleased and surprised. After all, this was no more strenuous than housework. She was reproached, too, for not showing enough initiative; but while accepting this criticism, she didn't know how to take the initiative.

At the meeting that evening, Sister Zhu called on them to go all out to complete an urgent order for ten thousand transmitters within seven days. A representative from the factory for which they were making the parts spoke after her. Producing a crumpled piece of paper from his pocket, he reeled off a whole list of figures, reminding Jinglan of the way she made up the accounts each evening. Except that the figures he quoted were so much bigger. At first she didn't listen very hard or grasp what he was driving at; but the look of concentration on his face reminded her of Mingfa. Whatever had Mingfa been writing that morning? Her husband had sat scribbling on the same sort of crumpled paper, wearing the same look of intense concentration. No doubt he'd be going off somewhere just like this representative to urge people to put on another spurt. But what made them behave like this? In the hope of understanding their secret, she started listening carefully.

When the meeting was opened to discussion, although Jinglan sat there without saying a word she agreed with what several of the others said. In the past, she'd neither spoken nor thought very hard. And for once the meeting broke up before she finished her sewing — of the two pairs of socks she had mended only one and a half.

It was after ten by the time Jinglan got home, and Mingfa and the boys were sound asleep. She didn't feel like going to bed or like working either. She sat down at the table. Her head was chock-a-block with ideas, but when she sat down to sort them out her mind went blank.

The table was strewn with the notes Mingfa had scribbled on crumpled pieces of paper filled with careful diagrams of every description. But he had crossed all of them out. A cross was scrawled over the first, over the second, over twenty-four altogether.

"He takes such pains. He's not the sort for whom 'anything will do'." Jinglan smoothed out the papers and stacked them together, her heart full again.

Someone was knocking at the gate of Number 16 next door. Sister Zhu was back. She always returned late like this, calling so loudly for someone to open the door that the whole sleeping lane suddenly came to life. She was knocking and shouting now at the same time. Her husband was a skilled electrician, also the sort who forgets to eat when he's on a job. Though he answered as soon as Sister Zhu started calling, she went on shouting just the same. Her voice sounded louder than ever because it was night.

"Here we are killing ourselves with work while you take it easy, turning in so early!"

With a creak the door opened and her husband said, "Well, well! Aren't you terrific! You make as much fuss every evening over that spot of work you do as if you'd just passed the palace examination!"

"What's that? Do you look down on what we do?" Sister Zhu sounded belligerent, but there was indescribable satisfaction in her voice.

"How dare I! I count it a great honour to be able to open the door for you every night."

Sister Zhu gave a peal of laughter, then the door creaked shut and quiet descended once again in the lane.

Jinglan stood up and opened the window. She took a deep breath, feeling her heart very heavy.

She got up no later than Sister Zhu and went to bed no earlier. Sister Zhu worked hard, but she was no slacker either; and Mingfa was as good if not better than Sister Zhu's husband. Why did the two of them hit it off so well, but not she and Mingfa? Why? . . .

The lane was dark and silent, with no one about. Only the light from her window and Sister Zhu's fell on the opposite wall. On that wall was a slogan in big characters, still clear and distinct, written to farewell the workers who had gone to help industry in other parts of the country. "Give your youth to the motherland!" The black characters on the red wall looked stronger and prouder than ever in the lamplight.

Jinglan looked over her shoulder at Mingfa, stretched out on his side fast asleep. The sight touched her — he must have tired himself out today. But thinking with a pang how little she meant to him now, she made haste to turn out the light and lie down herself. Sister Zhu's laughter, the big shrimps, the crosses on Mingfa's papers, the figures quoted by the workers' representative and the slogan "Give your youth to the motherland!"

— all these converged as if trying to convey something to her. Troubled at heart, she mulled matters over for a time. Finally two figures gripped her attention — seven and ten thousand — they had been repeated so often at today's meeting. In seven days they must finish ten thousand transmitters.

The fingers of the clock were approaching twelve as a tram rumbled past on its way to the terminus. Another ordinary Sunday had ended.

The next day at work Jinglan plied her task as usual, scarcely raising her head. But whereas usually her mind was a blank or her thoughts strayed from one subject to another, today she was obsessed by a single idea: ten thousand transmitters must be finished in seven days. She felt she was progressing too slowly, but instead of speeding up she broke into a sweat. Sister Zhu was not in the workshop but squatting outside in the yard by herself carefully examining an old electric fan.

"Doesn't she care?" marvelled Jinglan. When their shift ended, she went to see what Sister Zhu was doing. The latter liked to chatter and joke, but she answered gravely and quietly:

"I'm trying to make a machine. If we can mechanize the process of removing the rubber from the insulated wires that will speed things up. I saw a machine like that at the last industrial exhibition."

"A machine? . . ." Jinglan's thoughts flew to Mingfa's papers marked with crosses. "Can we make machines? . . ."

"Why not?" Sister Zhu frowned thoughtfully. "We need a round press this size for the machine. A wooden one would do. Have you any ideas?"

"I? . . ." Jinglan shook her head. Then she thought it over, glanced at Sister Zhu and suggested timidly: "We've part of a round tree trunk in our wood-pile at home. Shall I fetch it and try planing it?"

"Yes, do!" Sister Zhu's voice rose again.

"I'll fetch it then and have a try." Jinglan hurried home and pulled the round chunk of wood out of the stack. Putting it aside, she run to the canteen to buy rice and vegetables, then hastily wiped and set the table, and told Dabao and his brother to start dinner when their father came back. This done, she took the wood to their workshop.

She and Sister Zhu planed and sand-papered the wood. They had blisters on their hands before they finished. Jinglan was much later home than usual and much more tired, but she felt an unusual satisfaction.

The boys told her that they and their father had eaten and he had gone back to the works to help the night shift. Sitting down to eat, she discovered that Mingfa had left a great deal of the meat and vegetables for her. The boys, watching her, told her their father had left her the best. "Oh!" Jinglan's pleasure gave way to a vague sense of sadness. All her delight in the wooden press had vanished.

She went back to work the next day wondering if the press would do or not. Hurrying into the workshop yard, she noticed a crowd around a big red wall-newspaper. Never too interested in these bulletins, she pushed her way through the rest to find Sister Zhu. Failing, she was turning away when she saw with surprise her own name on the red paper. "Why's that? What have I done? . . ." She slipped through the crowd to read the announcement carefully. The wall-newspaper praised her and Sister Zhu for their boldness of thought and action in introducing technical innovations. Special mention was made of the fact that she had fetched the wood on her own initiative. At the same time they were wished speedy success so as to further ensure the completion of the ten thousand transmitters ordered. Jinglan's cheeks burned, her heart thumped. All this praise for simply planing a piece of wood! The others had spotted her and gathered round, all calling out at the same time. She could not catch exactly what each said, but she understood the general drift: they hoped the machine would be finished as quickly as possible to take the place of manual labour, raise working efficiency and speed up the completion of those ten thousand transmitters. That would show that housewives were not only hard-working but could use their heads, and their little workshop would be able to do its part like a real factory. Looking at their eager faces, Jinglan nodded again and again, but could not speak.

She had chopped up plenty of firewood in her life, but no one had said a word whether she made a good or bad job of it. If the wood was damp and didn't burn well, so that the rice cooked slowly, at the worst that delayed their family meal a little. But today. . . . It suddenly dawned on Jinglan that instead of chopping firewood yesterday she had been making a press for a machine, contributing her mite to socialist construction. . . .

"Wool-gathering again?" Sister Zhu grabbed her from behind. "I called you loudly enough, but you didn't hear. Come on quick. That press won't do."

"It won't do?" This blow chased all other thoughts from Jinglan's head. She realized how much depended on their success. Running to the scene of their experiment with Sister Zhu, she gave her whole mind to studying the problem.

The wooden press was rather hard, with the result that when it clamped down it snapped the insulated wires completely. Sister Zhu proposed fixing a thick layer of rubber over it, and Jinglan approved. They found a faulty bicycle tyre and fitted it on the press, but when the machine went into action it exerted pressure in some parts but not in others because the tyre had grooves — that was no good.

"I'll go to the junk stall and see if they've any smooth thick rubber." With a definite solution in mind, Jinglan knew what to do. She and Sister Zhu divided forces. The latter stayed there to prepare the other parts while Jinglan went out to find rubber.

The sun moved from the east to overhead, from overhead to the west. The canteen served lunch, then cooked supper. When six o'clock struck, the menu was written on a board in the canteen and the meal began to be served. Dabao and Erbao searched the lane frantically for their mother, while Sister Zhu at their heels loudly asked all she met if they'd seen Jinglan. Jinglan had not come home for lunch. She had stopped there jubilantly that afternoon, having bought a flat, thick length of rubber; but unable to fit it smoothly on to the press, she had disappeared again.

Indeed, at that very moment Jinglan was squatting in front of a cobbler's stall, watching his repeated attempts to fit the rubber on. It was as thick as two silver dollars. Skilled as he was, the cobbler couldn't make it lie flat.

Towards dusk, the sky clouded over, the wind grew

chill. Passers-by hastened their steps. But Jinglan and the cobbler were perspiring. He seemed to have reached the end of his patience, and she was growing desperate. She had never known such a heavy responsibility, such fearful anxiety. She encouraged and pleaded with the cobbler, but after looking up at the sky he dropped his hammer into the tool box and handed her the press and rubber, saying, "It's no use. The rubber is too thick. And I've got to pack up now."

Jinglan looked up. It was growing dark. She suddenly remembered supper. The canteen tickets were in her pocket. Picking up her things, she raced home. Never in over a dozen years had she failed her family like this before. She knew it was of no great consequence: Mingfa wouldn't make an issue of it and it wouldn't really hurt the boys. Still, she was frantic.

When she reached home, she found Mingfa still out while the boys were in the middle of a piping hot meal. Dabao told her that Aunt Zhu had gone to a meeting, leaving word that if it ended early she would drop in. It was Sister Zhu who had bought supper for them.

"Well!" Since Mingfa was out, Jinglan relaxed a little; but at once something else started preying on her mind. "What are we going to do if the rubber can't be fitted on?" Hungry as she was, she just held her bowl in her hands without touching the rice.

Outside, some of her work mates were asking Dabao:

"Is your mother back yet?"

"Is the press finished now?"

More distraught than ever, Jinglan hurriedly finished a bowl of rice, told Dabao to put his younger brother to bed, and went back to the workshop with the wooden press and rubber.

Alone there under the lamp, she whittled carefully at the rubber to thin it, and then tried fitting it on again. But the thickness was uneven — that wouldn't do. She tried again, whittling strip after strip. At the third failure, she gave up. In her mind's eye she saw the eager faces of the other women, the bright red wall-newspaper, the crumpled paper held by the workers' representative, his tone so trusting, and Sister Zhu's anxious expression.

"Tomorrow's the third day. What shall we do if we can't deliver that order in time!" With tears in her eyes, Jinglan sat there like a statue. A clock somewhere struck twelve. "Mingfa must be back now. I wonder if the boys have kicked off their bedding. . . ." The old worries occupied her for an instant, only to be driven away by the job in hand.

"What can I do? I must think of a way out." Jinglan wiped her eyes, but fresh tears welled up immediately. Through her tears, the rubber looked thicker and more cumbersome than ever.

"Jinglan!" Starting at the sound of her name called out in the quiet spring night, she looked round to see Mingfa standing in the doorway.

"Mingfa! . . ." Somehow she couldn't hold back the tears which coursed down her cheeks.

"What's the matter, Jinglan?" He walked over.

Despite her anxiety, Jinglan was so happy to see him that she wiped her eyes and told him the whole trouble. Mingfa's face cleared. Without a word he picked up the wood and rubber, held them up against each other and suggested, "Why not just make a press out of this thick rubber?"

"Yes! Oh, yes!" Jinglan's eyes brightened. Then she added, "But how can we make it absolutely round?"

"I'll fix it on the lathe in our works. That's easy."

That rubber had given her so much trouble, however, that she still had her doubts. But before she could voice them, Mingfa hurried her out of the door.

The road was quiet, the street lamps were swaying a little in the wind. Since the last tram had gone, they walked side by side in the middle of the road.

"We need that as soon as it's light. Can you manage it in time?" she asked softly. But her voice carried clearly through the quiet night.

"Oh, yes, it'll be ready all right," was his confident reply. Jinglan said nothing, unable to believe this till she saw it.

A snack bar was still open and lit up, but with no customers inside. Either because he was hungry or to emphasize that there was plenty of time, Mingfa led his wife in without consulting her, sat down and ordered two bowls of noodles.

Time was so short, yet he'd dropped in here for a snack. Jinglan didn't altogether approve. Still, she didn't want her husband to go hungry. She sat there on tenterhooks, glancing at the electric clock every few minutes, her problem weighing on her mind.

It seemed a long time before the noodles were served. As usual she transferred the meat on top to her husband's bowl, then lowered her head to eat. She could not tell what the noodles tasted like, for a rubber press was revolving in her head, one moment oval, the next elongated, before regaining its original shape. . . .

"You've had a hard day, Jinglan. You must make a good meal."

Jinglan suddenly became aware of chopsticks reaching over, a big red shrimp held between them.

She quivered and raised her head to see her husband watching her with kind, loving eyes.

How well she knew that look in his eyes! But, strangely enough, this seemed even more loving than the look she knew. Tears of confusion filled her eyes again. That invisible, intangible "barrier" had vanished completely.

Jinglan was too overwhelmed to eat for some minutes; but this surge of excitement receded just as swiftly as it had come. Before she could analyse this sudden development, she heard the clear resonant voice of the big clock in the Customs House by the Huangpu River — it was one o'clock. Coming to herself with a start, she reflected that the main problem wasn't yet solved. A great deal depended on whether or not that machine could go into action first thing in the morning. She glanced at her husband, who was looking straight at her. This time there were no tears or shame in Jinglan's eyes. As if prompting him to hurry, she hastily shelled the large red shrimp, blushing to remember those she had bought on Sunday.

Jinglan left the snack bar holding the wood and rubber, walking by her husband's side in the middle of the road. The whole city was asleep. Only the great shadows of trees were stirring by the roadside.

"Can you guarantee to make it work, Mingfa?" she asked.

"Silly! What do you think my job is? I can twist steel into any shape I want. This rubber is child's play."

"You guarantee it?"

"Of course."

They walked on close together, not saying a word but very close in spirit. Working for the same end, they were travelling the same road.

It was late and the wind was high. Suddenly thunder rumbled and it started to rain. Mingfa took off his jacket and put it round his wife's shoulders. They walked on more swiftly.

The first thunder of spring had sounded. Though the wind was keen, Jinglan felt gloriously warm.

October 1959

Translated by Gladys Yang

The Maternity Home

THE sunset glow deepened and then faded, till only faint smudges of cloud were left on the horizon like the brush-strokes of an ink painting. The little pink flowers on the fence round the maternity home blurred and were lost to sight. Evening had set in.

With a carrying-pole and two buckets, Aunt Tan filled the big water vat. Then, without pausing for breath, she bustled off to prepare supper for her two patients. Though getting on in years, she prided herself on being able to keep on the go all day. When supper was over, she went into the middle room. As she snapped on the electric light, this combined office and delivery room appeared more spacious. Every object in it seemed to glow: the smooth white sheet on the bed and the white screen round it, the white desk, white walls and ceiling. . . . It was wonderful the way the electric light made everything seem so much whiter and smarter. Half-closing her eyes, she looked round her before hurrying over to the stove to stir the fire and put the sterilizer on to boil, dumping all her used instruments into it.

Her patients were sleeping peacefully. The water in the sterilizer had not yet come to the boil. Aunt Tan turned off the light. In the darkness, distant noises seemed more distinct. The electric pump across the river was thudding away, from the club came the sound of the wireless, turned on full blast. Out on the sports ground the young fellows of the shock brigade were playing ball; she could hear their staccato whistle. These sounds gave Aunt Tan a feeling of satisfaction.

When the country was first liberated, who had heard of a maternity home, sterilizer, lying-in or electric lights in a village? In those days child-birth was a trip through the valley of death. Back in 1950, when Aunt Tan's daughter-in-law had her baby, the midwife expelled the afterbirth by stamping on the mother's abdomen. In 1956 when they had an agricultural co-operative, she was sent by Chairman Du, now Party secretary of the commune, to learn the new scientific method of delivery at the town hospital. But popularizing the new method hadn't been easy! Expectant mothers and their families did not believe in her; she was given the cold shoulder. Old-style midwives spread lies about her. Lack of experience made her task doubly difficult. Once, a patient who was having a difficult labour was sent to the hospital too late, and the baby died. This slip caused a great deal of talk and trouble. One of the old-fashioned midwives, Granny Pan, accused Aunt Tan of killing the baby. That made the poor mother more indignant and the scandal grew. Angry and hurt, Aunt Tan hid her face at home. Many infants had died at the hands of the old midwives, but their families made no trouble, merely blaming fate. Yet now, for one little slip, they were tearing her apart. Unable to stand such accusations, she went with tears in her eyes to Chairman Du. He was at the threshing-floor, seeing to the soaking of seeds before planting. Having heard her out, he rubbed his big calloused hands and said gravely but gently: "Our generation has a task that's far from simple, aunty. We're going to change society and keep on changing it! Things are developing at tremendous speed, but old ideas and old ways die hard. Our work is making a revolution and our study is making a revolution too. What we can't do we must learn; what we don't understand we must find out."

Later Secretary Du announced that a maternity home was to be set up and put aside three rooms for this purpose. And there Aunt Tan made a desk with her own hands, got hold of a high bed for deliveries and five other beds for a ward. The three ordinary rooms had become a clean and peaceful maternity home.

"Why, it's nearly as good as a hospital!" The first night Aunt Tan was too excited to sleep. She thought back over the years since she was widowed at thirty-nine to her present post in this maternity home . . . as what? It was hard to find the right word to describe her position. At last she silently settled on "obstetrician".

Here in this maternity home which was "nearly as good as a hospital", Aunt Tan learned to give injections, make prenatal examinations, take the blood pressure, get specimens of blood, put in stitches and remove them. Whenever a doctor was fetched from town for minor operations, she served as his assistant, winning praise for her composure and skill. In fact one or two doctors went so far as to suggest that she could learn to do these simple operations herself. Aunt Tan smiled with amused pride at the thought that the doctors imagined her little maternity home able to cope with cases meant for the town hospitals.

The water bubbled merrily in the sterilizer, matching the contentment in the midwife's heart. Suddenly the door burst open. Turning on the light, Aunt Tan saw a dark, ruddy-faced girl at the door. She had a roll of bedding over one shoulder, an oxygen tank under one arm and looked hot and flushed.

"Remember me, aunt?" asked the girl with a smile.

"If it isn't Hemei!" Hemei, the daughter of Mrs Zhang, had just graduated from the obstetrician's course in town, Aunt Tan and Mrs Zhang had been friends since girlhood. With a glad cry, Aunt Tan relieved Hemei of the bedding, then made the girl sit down.

Hemei's dark oval face glowed pink under the electric lamp as her big shining eyes surveyed the room with interest. "I've been sent to work here, aunt," said she. Picking up her bedding roll, she hoisted it to her shoulder and then put it down in a far corner of the room. The bulky bedding must have weighed at least eighty catties, but it rested as lightly as paper on her strong young shoulders. Returning to her seat, Hemei begged to be told all about the maternity home.

"Very well, dear." Aunt Tan approved of this serious, grown-up approach. "I'm so glad you've come, child. You're going to be my right hand. I expect you know a good deal about us already. Our home takes care of all the pregnant women in the two work brigades round here. There's a Mrs Zhou who helps here too. In the two years since this home started, we've delivered three hundred and fifty-six babies, and every one of them safely." Aunt Tan warmed as she got on to the subject of babies. Three hundred and fifty-six babies. It hadn't been easy. It had meant much anxiety and worry, particularly since the maternity home was unable to cope with the slightest complications. In many cases, Aunt Tan had to make a prompt decision either to send for the doctor or to rush the patient to hospital. The least slip might well cost a life. That was why she had emphasized every word of the last sentence.

"Listen child, we've a risky and heavy burden on our shoulders. In our two years' history we've not let a single accident happen. No harm came to any mother or child. A woman comes in alone but leaves with a baby in her arms. . . ." Since words were not enough to express what she felt, Aunt Tan stood up to show Hemei the whole home. They went first into the ward, a large room with five beds of various types and sizes. Two only were occupied but all were neatly made and stood in their proper place.

From time to time Hemei nodded her approval. "Aunt Tan, have we ever had difficult births?" she asked suddenly.

"Have we! That's where the worry comes in. As soon as there's any sign of complications, I have to go and telephone for the ambulance."

"Suppose there's no time?"

"Get on the phone and ask for a doctor."

"Where do we wash our hands?" asked Hemei presently.

"Wash our hands?" Aunt Tan was puzzled by the question. "In the wash basin of course." She felt slightly put out by all these questions. Still, she drew out all three drawers in her desk to exhibit their contents. But Hemei did not understand her pride in them. Cocking her head, her short plaits sticking out, she cast her eyes round the room, paying no attention to the medical instruments in the drawers.

"Of course, child, we can't compare with the big

hospitals in town." Aunt Tan spoke more sharply now, rather annoyed.

"Of course not," said Hemei, unaware of the implied reproach, as she pushed open a window to peer out into the darkness. The next moment she slipped out of the door, as if in search of something.

Slowly Aunt Tan closed the drawers one by one. She no longer had any desire to tell the girl anything or show off her treasures. "I'm wasting my breath on her," she thought with a sinking heart. "I may as well pack her off to bed early."

"I've found a way, aunt!" Hemei rushed in, her eyes dancing. "Listen, aunt, we can rig up a home-made running-water system. You know the commune nursery's already got running water for the kiddies. Our maternity home needs it even more. I've looked things over. The well's near enough, all we have to do is make a hole in the wall. . . ."

Aunt Tan had been staring at Hemei without a word. Now she interposed with, "Come and let me show you your bed." She went to the room on the east end and pointed to an empty bed. "You can sleep on Mrs Zhou's bed while she's away."

Aunt Tan's impression of Hemei during this first meeting as colleagues was not so good, though she could not put her finger on what was wrong. There was just something about the girl that disturbed her. All those questions about difficult births and complications. . . . Still, it was silly to let herself be annoyed by a mere child like Hemei.

"These youngsters!" thought Aunt Tan with a sigh. "They've had white rice in their bowls ever since they can remember. To have land to till and food to eat, to go to school or attend training courses are all things they take for granted. So are this maternity home, the electric light, tractors and everything. What do they know about hard times, bitterness or suffering? . . ." It would be wrong, though, to neglect the girl. She had better have a good talk with her. By the time she had banked up the stove, she discovered that Hemei was already in bed and her things tidied out of the way.

"Your mother must be pleased now you're back from training," said Aunt Tan, sitting down by the girl's bed.

"She is!" Under her warm quilt Hemei smiled with delight.

"It hasn't been easy, child. Now we've got everything: midwives, maternity homes . . . but in the old days having a baby was a real trial. You can't imagine what women then went through. Yet nowadays you young people sometimes find fault with this or that. It seems nothing's good enough for you. In our younger days we never dreamed of such a happy life. Young people should understand that life isn't all fun."

"You're right, aunt." There was a serious look on Hemei's glowing young face. Aunt Tan was reassured to see her words producing their desired effect. As she began to prepare for bed, she realized that the light in the outer room was still on. Hemei's question about running water had made her forget to turn it off. Aunt Tan hurried out, looked the room over again and put a few things in order before she turned off the light.

"Now we've got electric light, our life is getting better and better. . . ." Going back, she found Hemei already asleep, her short plaits sticking out at an angle from her head and one hand thrust under the pillow.

"They were born at the right time," Aunt Tan told

herself as she watched the girl's guileless face so peaceful in sleep. Suddenly Hemei turned over and muttered, "Let's fix up the running water tomorrow, aunt. . . ." The next moment she was fast asleep again.

"She's even dreaming about the running water! These youngsters are all alike." Aunt Tan shook her head, turned off the light and got into bed.

There was a pale white ring round the bright full moon. Though the shadows cast by the trees were motionless and not even a leaf was stirring, it looked as if there would be wind the next day.

Early the next morning, Aunt Tan felt irritated the moment she stepped out of her room. It seemed Hemei had got the two patients out of bed and was teaching them exercises. The three of them were very merry, laughing and giggling as they bent their backs and swung their legs.

There was nothing extraordinary about post-natal exercises, in fact Aunt Tan had seen them done in the town hospital some time back. But she had no intention of introducing exercises into her maternity home. She didn't care to see a woman, particularly a new mother, stamping her feet and swinging her arms like that; she for one would never be able to learn such undignified motions. Besides, the villagers had always believed in sleep, rest and good food to help a woman recover after child-birth. Exercises had never been considered of the slightest importance. But here was Hemei, just after her arrival, introducing hospital ways without even a "by your leave". Aunt Tan was very put out. She marched in to stop them.

"This is better for them than any medicine, aunt," said Hemei, smiling unperturbed.

"This is fun!" cried one of the patients. "It's better than lying flat all day." The other patient also voted for exercises. Aunt Tan felt more put out to find both of them in favour of this new-fangled idea. "If you're all for it, go ahead," she concluded with a forced smile.

Usually Aunt Tan kept on the move from morning till night. But today she could not settle down to work. She'd pick up a task in the office but before it was done find herself walking into the kitchen. The three younger women were having a gay time in the ward. She could hear Hemei's "one, two, three and four!" and the two patients laughing and moving about.

A fresh wind seemed to have blown into the quiet maternity home, disturbing its order and peace. Aunt Tan picked up a bamboo basket and walked quickly out. Wanting an excuse to go out, she had decided to buy eggs for the home from the poultry farm.

She walked slowly. There were only two *li* to go. Her head felt empty, yet something was weighing on her mind. She could not tell the reason for her depression. "Ah, the older I get the more discontented I grow. What is there for me to feel unhappy about?" she asked herself sternly.

The sun would soon be appearing at the horizon, the cotton field was a stretch of green. A few belated flowers dotted the green cotton plants with white; before long it would be time to pick the cotton. People were out working already. All the women knew Aunt Tan and hailed her from a distance. One called out that baby had been weaned, another that Afang had learned to walk. Their friendly greetings were balm to Aunt Tan's heart. She kept nodding and smiling, calling or waving back. Pride and happiness dispelled all her discontent.

Outside the poultry farm, a pond covered by duckweed made a patch of luscious green. As Aunt Tan drew near, she saw Granny Pan tiptoeing round the pond.

"Whatever is she doing?" Aunt Tan wondered. When she called out, Granny Pan was too intent on something at the edge of the pond even to turn her head. Suddenly she pounced. At the same time a frog landed with a splash in the water.

"You frightened it off." Granny Pan turned reproachfully.

"Trying to get a few frogs to fry, Granny Pan?"

"It's for our hens." She walked with Aunt Tan to the poultry farm, carrying a jar in which frogs were croaking lustily.

"Your hens are spoiled, granny. Eating frogs, indeed!" Amused as Aunt Tan was by the sight of the white-haired old woman holding a jar of frogs, she respected her determination to do her work well.

"Do you know we are having a competition?" Granny Pan spoke as if she were sharing a delightful secret. "Each of us takes care of two hundred and fifty hens and we see whose are the best fed and lay the most eggs. You must give the hens proper food if you want them to lay well. The best thing for them is caterpillars. But with the campaign to protect the trees and insecticide sprayed over every single leaf, there aren't any caterpillars left. I have to make do by boiling a few mussels from the creek and these. At least that gives them meat of a sort." Granny Pan chuckled.

Aunt Tan was struck by the kindly, shrewd expression on the old woman's wrinkled face. She marvelled

at the difference made by a change in her way of thinking. Granny Pan, as an old-fashioned midwife, had
looked hard and miserable. By popularizing the new
method of midwifery, Aunt Tan had called Granny
Pan's wrath down on her head. The old woman had
often come to her door cursing wildly or weeping. Now
she was transformed. Her eyes were shining, her face
gentle . . . she had changed into a lovable person.

In the yard of the poultry farm was a huge chart
showing the progress of the emulation campaign. When
Aunt Tan came out with her eggs she stood looking at
the chart for quite a while. The red arrow under
Granny Pan's name had soared proudly to the top.
"Changed? Yes, Granny Pan has changed." Something
disturbed Aunt Tan's peace of mind again. She was
both glad and upset at the same time.

All the way back, she kept turning over in her mind
the way things were changing. This friend's son was
learning to drive a truck, that one's daughter was training to be a tractor driver. Maybe tomorrow Granny
Pan would become an advanced worker, and what
would happen the day after there was no telling. . . .
Now the fields were irrigated by a network of channels
and ditches, the pumps thudded day and night, electric
light had been installed — what would come next? . . .
It dawned on her with absolute clarity that one day
was no longer like another, changes were occurring with
every passing day.

Yes, all around her was undergoing a rapid, tremendous change.

When Aunt Tan reached the maternity home she
stood transfixed on the threshold. The office which
she had so carefully swept and dusted that very morning

was littered with sawdust and bits of bamboo. The benches were upturned, and her wooden rice barrel had a hole in it near the bottom. Several newly cut bamboos lay across the floor. A fire just outside the door was still smouldering. What was more, a big opening had been made in one of the lovely white walls and there stood Hemei trying to connect two bamboo pipes.

Hemei had discovered that the well from which Aunt Tan fetched water with her pole and buckets was on higher ground than the maternity home. She had therefore brought the water directly into the room with bamboo pipes. She cried out at sight of Aunt Tan: "Come and look at our running water!"

"Running water? . . ." Aunt Tan righted a bench and sat down heavily. She was tired out. All this was too much for her. Hemei, who had worked feverishly on the new device, had expected Aunt Tan to be surprised and pleased with the running water. Now, wiping her perspiring face she waited, but Aunt Tan said not a word. Hemei was bewildered.

"My dear child," Aunt Tan spoke at last. "The villages don't have all the comforts of the towns. Don't let us get so soft that we can't stand the weight of the carrying-pole. I don't think that's right."

"I agree," said Hemei seriously. "But, aunt, the villages won't always be back-country. If we can rig up a running water system but don't, sticking to our carrying-pole, that's nothing to be proud of. It's backward. . . ."

"Hemei's said it, Aunt Tan," chimed in one of the patients bluntly. "It's backward not to make improvements when we can. This new arrangement is more convenient, sanitary and scientific. I mean to popularize it when I go back."

"Of course!" answered Aunt Tan, struck by the familiar words. She had used the same words herself three years ago of the new midwifery methods. How many people had she told, "This is sanitary and scientific!" She had said it to the women, their husbands and mothers-in-law — most of all to Granny Pan. Now she eyed the new water pipes, the oxygen tank Hemei had brought, and the girl's shining eyes. Her gaze came to rest on the electric lamp. . . .

Inwardly shaken as by some invisible storm, Aunt Tan suddenly understood the feelings of Granny Pan three years ago: why the older woman had raged and pleaded, had appeared hard and yet pathetic. Granny Pan had been frightened by the fact — yet refused to admit it — that she was behind the times.

"Am I now like Granny Pan three years ago?"

The sky darkened. The trees danced in the wind predicted by the white ring round the moon the previous night. Aunt Tan stood up wanting something to do and mechanically picked up her carrying-pole. Just then Hemei came back cheering happily, having completed joining the pipes. Aunt Tan silently abandoned the carrying-pole.

"Aunt Tan!" a breathless voice called from the door. A man stood there supporting a woman big with child. "My wife's very near her time now."

Aunt Tan jumped up, all energy. Hemei abandoned her pipes to lend a hand. The new patient, Caidi, was quickly settled in bed while the other two went back to their ward. The maternity home was its old self again.

"Reckless scamp!" Aunt Tan turned, beaming, to Caidi's husband. "Letting her come here on foot!"

He smiled foolishly, then solemnly told Aunt Tan that he was now a lorry driver and had brought his wife in the lorry, parked outside. He was on his way to fetch mats as the commune had been alerted for a storm that was brewing. After a few more words of thanks he left.

Now, Caidi and her husband had played a memorable part in Aunt Tan's career. Late one night, soon after Aunt Tan came back from her midwifery course, Caidi's husband had come for her on his bicycle. In those days she was inexperienced and her heart had thumped when she remembered that it was Caidi's first baby. The night was cold and it was drizzling. Sitting on the carrier, Aunt Tan started shivering. The young husband pedalled like one possessed at the thought of his impending fatherhood. What with him too impatient to look where he was going and Aunt Tan behind him shaking like a leaf, the bicycle crashed and both riders were thrown quite a distance. Aunt Tan's leg was badly scratched. Now, that firstborn was four but Aunt Tan still called his father "reckless scamp".

"You're driving a lorry now, remember! If you're still reckless you'll land in real trouble." Aunt Tan delivered this parting shot at the retreating back of the young husband, while Caidi smiled behind the screen. Aunt Tan was tempted to tell Hemei the story so that she would know how the new midwifery had been introduced four years ago. Hemei, however, merely smiled but asked no questions. She put on a white smock, turned on the newly installed running water to wash her hands and then sat down beside Caidi to massage her back, teach her the breathing exercises and prepare her for a painless childbirth.

Aunt Tan watched all this with a new feeling of peace, annoyed neither by the running water nor by Hemei's professional movements. The young couple's arrival had reminded her of achievements of which she could be proud, and of her hard work in popularizing the new method. She carefully sterilized her hands with alcohol and was soon telling Hemei about Caidi's first-born, even showing her the scar on her leg. Hemei doubled up with laughter.

The sky darkened. Outside, the wind rose. Loudspeakers in the fields and on the village roads burst out together with a message from Party Secretary Du. He urged the commune members to cover the vegetable patches as quickly as possible and to shield the cotton plants properly from the wind. They must not lose a single boll of cotton. All the commune's men and machines started a battle against the wind. Lorries tooted, excited voices were heard and the loudspeaker poured forth words of encouragement: these sounds were carried into the maternity home by gusts of strong wind at one moment but in the next the wind veered and all was silent. It was warm and cozy in the delivery room. The electric lamp shed a steady light over the delivery table, the two midwives, young and old, standing beside it and the mother waiting patiently to give birth.

Like a veteran of a hundred battles, Aunt Tan stood by, confident and strong. The woman in labour trusted her completely. And Aunt Tan responded to this trust like a real soldier, like the midwives in big hospitals, waiting at her post for the exciting and happy moment of delivery.

Resting peacefully between her labour pains, Caidi opened her eyes to glance at the bright electric light. She smiled as she thought of the difference between her present surroundings and that time her firstborn came into the world. She also dreamed of her children's future.

"There's only four years between them. But don't you think, aunt, this new baby will be much luckier than its brother?"

"The old folk would say it is born in a lucky time," Aunt Tan said excitedly.

The wind whirled and howled. By contrast, the room seemed particularly quiet. Hemei kept on massaging the patient's back. Caidi began to show signs of fatigue. She yawned and seemed to be falling asleep. Her contractions were tapering off.

Both old-fashioned and new-style midwives know that when a woman starts to yawn towards the end of her labour, it spells trouble. If the labour is unduly prolonged, the baby has to be delivered with forceps, otherwise it may stifle and the mother's life may be endangered. Delivery by forceps is a simple operation, requiring not more than ten minutes at the most. But Aunt Tan stood up abruptly at this juncture. "I'll go to the phone," she announced, making for the door. Hemei ran after her, but she had vanished into the darkness and the howling wind.

Aunt Tan ran towards the brigade office as fast as she could. The wind tore at her clothes and shrieked into her ears. This was not the first time she had rushed to the telephone, she had always felt that it was the right thing to do. The electric light was shining on the white bed on which the patient lay. Yes, everything was as it should be, except poor Aunt Tan, who couldn't do anything but rush to the telephone. It had been like this from the beginning. They now had electricity, lorries and tractors, yet she still rushed for the telephone when all the patient needed was a ten-minute operation. For the first time Aunt Tan felt almost ashamed to call up the hospital.

The sky was black. The wind roared through the deep, dark night. Secretary Du's voice carried distinctly across the fields, over the roof-tops and along the country roads. "Comrades, the wind wants to rob us of our cotton, but we won't let it! We'll safeguard every single plant. We mustn't let a single boll be blown off. . . ." To Aunt Tan, he seemed to be whispering: "Our generation has a task that's far from simple, aunty. We're going to change society and keep on changing it. Things are developing at tremendous speed, but old ideas and old ways die hard. . . ." Aunt Tan wiped the sweat from her forehead and slowed down.

Two columns of light pierced the black road in front. A lorry loaded with mats flashed past. The first batch of lorry drivers trained by the commune were at their post. The first tractor drivers were at their post, the first trained obstetrician. . . . A young ruddy face was suddenly before her mind's eye, a smiling face with short plaits sticking out at angles. "Hemei!" Aunt Tan stopped. When she left the maternity home, Hemei's young face had been calm and composed. Yes, the first trained obstetrician was at her post too. She had not rushed into the night for the telephone. Aunt Tan turned and ran back to the maternity home, which now had its own doctor, had entered a new stage. Aunt Tan saw clearly now.

The wind pushed her along with such force that her feet barely touched the ground. When she reached the home, Hemei was putting on a sterilized gown. She was not as calm as Aunt Tan had imagined, but somewhat tense, although not really nervous. Caidi was still dozing.

"I don't think we should wait any longer, aunt," said Hemei in a worried tone.

"Hurry then, child." There was infinite warmth in Aunt Tan's voice.

"I'm a little nervous. I've only done this twice and both times another doctor was with me."

"Don't you worry, child. I'm with you now. The first time is always a little frightening, but don't we always get over it all right?" Aunt Tan washed and sterilized her hands, took the rubber gloves from the drawer and helped Hemei put them on.

All kinds of emotion had welled up in her heart: excitement, happiness, a touch of envy and considerable self-reproach. Watching Hemei, a mask over her mouth, pacing back and forth getting things ready, clanking the forceps, Aunt Tan felt this was in keeping with the bright electric light overhead.

"Caidi hit on the truth just now. Her firstborn is not as lucky as this second one, and Hemei is luckier than I. All that talk about lucky hours and horoscopes is nonsense but it's much better to be born now, to begin life today."

The wind raged outside but Secretary Du's clear voice still sounded in her ears: ". . . Our work is making a revolution and our study is making a revolution too."

"No, we older folk should take the lead. I want to give a lead. I can learn, Secretary Du, and I want to learn. I mean to work for the revolution. . . ." Straightening her back, Aunt Tan walked towards Hemei. Her legs felt as shaky as when she delivered her first baby.

"Hemei, let me learn to do this."

Hemei noticed the timid appeal in Aunt Tan's face as she stood firmly before her. In that instant she understood the whole history of the maternity home, the struggle involved to introduce scientific midwifery. She pictured Aunt Tan on a bicycle carrier at midnight on her way to deliver a baby; she remembered how proudly Aunt Tan turned on the electric light. . . .

Hemei felt like hugging the older woman who was so young and strong. But there was no time to say more than, "You're right, aunt, this is not a bit difficult. We'll do it together this time. You'll be able to do it alone next time."

Aunt Tan turned on the running water, washed her hands again carefully, and rubbed them with alcohol before going to the delivery table.

Everything went smoothly though Aunt Tan ceased to be aware of the whiteness of the bed, the brightness of the lamp and the howling of the wind. She saw only Hemei's skilful hands moving rapidly but with assurance and heard only her requests for this instrument or that. Suddenly, a newborn infant's cry pierced the air. It was a boy, another little "reckless scamp".

When Aunt Tan straightened up, Hemei's strong

young arms held her close. "Aunt!" Her eyes were bright with tears of joy.

"Good work, aunt!" said the two patients coming out of the ward. Aunt Tan sat down with a smile. She looked up at the lamp, which was so bright. This light hanging there so serenely was not merely a means of illumination, there was invisible force in its radiance. Aunt Tan seemed to hear again Secretary Du's voice: "Our generation has a task that's far from simple. We're going to change society and keep on changing it. . . ."

"Don't you worry, Party secretary," Aunt Tan reassured him silently. "I know our work is making a revolution and our study too. So let's go ahead and learn."

The wind, as if conquered by that firm strong voice, began to withdraw. The night became quiet again. The hands of the clock showed midnight. This quiet maternity home, together with all the villages and towns of China, moved forward into a new day — a glorious day never known before.

April 1960

Translated by Tang Sheng

A Third Visit to Yanzhuang

THERE was no wind that night, but snow kept falling. It drifted down leisurely to drop noiselessly on the road, on the winter wheat, in the trenches. Lamplights flashed in villages near and far; here and there occasional sparks floated from cottage chimneys. The people and the army along the Huaihai front were happily spending the last few hours of 1948.

I had just been to the front lines to congratulate the fighters on their brave deeds and to wish them a happy New Year. I walked back alone on the snow-covered ground, what I had seen was still vivid in my mind: Light grey planes of Chiang Kai-shek hastily parachuting boxes to their besieged troops, then hastily flying away. Enemy soldiers in our encirclement ran riot even as the boxes were still drifting down, rushing like starving mad dogs from their dugouts to snatch and fight over them. In fortifications decorated with pine branches and red flowers, our fighters sat watching and commenting on their behaviour. One fighter, a husky big fellow, said humorously: "Why do they fight over them? They ought to put all the boxes together and then divide them up!"

"You ought to be their commander-in-chief," remarked another fighter.

"I'm not boasting," the former said seriously. "If they made me their commander-in-chief, I'd see to it that they didn't go hungry. I'd say, 'Surrender your arms and you can cross over and eat big wheat cakes.' "

"Haha. . . ." Thunderous laughter broke out in the fortifications. Then another PLA company fired two shots at the scrambling enemy — to "make peace". This device was most effective. At the sound of the shots, all the fighting, wrestling and snatching ceased and every Kuomintang soldier scuttled back to his dugout. Our fighters burst into laughter which was interrupted by a sudden whistle. The cooking squad had brought them their New Year's Eve dinner, piping hot.

Narrowing his eyes, the big fellow bit into a white flour dumpling, and chewed it with relish. "This flour must have been sent from our Jiaodong," he said.

"It's from Jinan!"

"It's from Taixing!"

"It's from. . . ."

Ah! Snow-white flour. Biting into the snow-white dumplings, I recalled a small village a thousand *li* away and a simple village woman. She had said that she would have white flour milled and ready for me. This wheat flour might have come from Yanzhuang, I thought. It might have been sent by Shoulizi and Laichuan! I decided excitedly, "It was she. It was he."

It seemed to be snowing harder. The ground was a stretch of white. Someone had left a trail of deep footprints on the road, footprints made with large strides leading to the front line. I turned up the ear flaps of my army cap to let the snow-flakes caress my burning cheeks. I wanted to cool the excitement in my heart. But it was no use. My mind was in a tumult. Many connected and unconnected things, many clearly remembered and some half forgotten, all surged up together. . . .

Last year, 1947, when the *kaoliang* was turning red, I went to Yanzhuang for the first time with Comrade Ma of the mass work department of the military area. Yanzhuang had been liberated for some time, but its local armed forces were weak. Reactionary gangs, hand in glove with the landlords, often made trouble. They even came into the village at midnight with a chaff-chopper to look for our village cadres. So land reform work in this area was rather special. On the one hand, the peasants longed for land; on the other, they were hesitant and dared not ask for it. Our task was to help the government to try out land reform here on a small scale: We were to mobilize the masses, carry out land reform and organize the peasants' own "home guards" at the same time.

Yanzhuang was a fine place. In front and behind the village, level land stretched far into the distance, broken only by the faint lines of mountains on the horizon. When a district cadre took us to the village it was broad daylight, but the place was utterly silent, so silent that it made me uneasy. We went first to the home of Yan Laichuan, chairman of the peasants' association. He was a blunt fellow in his thirties. He and his father were repairing their courtyard wall when we entered. The sight of two people in army uniform stunned him. A little tense, he quickly took us into the room and closed his door with a bang. Then he greeted us, "How are you, comrades?"

The extraordinary silence of the village and the way Laichuan shut his door caused me to make a quick decision. I must get an art troupe to come and give a performance here the next day, to drive away this unpleasant silence with gongs and drums, songs and dances and let the people talk to us with their doors wide open.

As soon as Laichuan closed the door the room became so dark that we couldn't make out each other's faces. I heard Old Ma asking Laichuan straight-to-the-point questions: What was the situation of the dependable masses of the village, how many activists were there, and so on. After some time, I discovered that there was another source of light in the room. It came through the doorway behind me which led into another room. Light shone in through a paper window-pane there overlooking a large brick bed. A woman of twenty or so sat primly at one end of the brick bed beside the window. Obviously Laichuan's wife. Sitting in the light she was sewing with downcast eyes. She seemed not to notice at all that two strangers had come to her house. At the time I took her to be one of those quiet, docile women who paid no attention to anything which did not concern her.

Old Ma was telling Laichuan how to get in touch with the masses and develop activists, how to hold solidarity meetings and carry out land reform. Laichuan listened attentively. But suddenly I saw him frowning at something behind me. I turned and saw that the placid, quiet woman had left the brick bed and was leaning against the door frame listening to what was being said. Even though Laichuan knitted his brows and glared at her she pretended not to notice. She stayed where she was and listened to Old Ma. When I turned to look she smiled at me in a friendly manner, then walked away softly. When Old Ma finished about how the poor peasants and hired hands should unite to struggle against the landlords and share out the land, Laichuan rose immediately and rolled up his sleeves. Pulling open the door with one hand, he said, "Right. Come what may, we'll drive it through!"

Light streamed into the room as soon as the door was opened. But outside, the village was still quiet. Neither dogs barked nor roosters crowed. Not a sound could be heard. Laichuan's father was still absorbed in repairing the wall. All this seemed to exert a sort of pressure on Laichuan. Veins showing on his forehead, he hesitated for a moment. "What if the masses don't follow us?" he asked.

"If we really arouse them, they will," Old Ma said with conviction.

I turned and found Laichuan's wife again quietly leaning against the door, a faint smile on her face.

That night, I stayed in Laichuan's house and shared a bed with his wife while Laichuan slept with his father in the outer room.

I did not like staying in this house particularly. The members of this family were all tongue-tied, as if they were bewitched. Laichuan's father, a small pipe clamped between his teeth all day long, worked and ate with his head down. He never said anything. As for Laichuan's wife, I never heard a sound from her either. Perhaps she was taciturn by nature, or had feudal notions of propriety. Laichuan himself was a bit shy with me because I was a woman. If he had something to discuss he would go to Old Ma. So I had only his six-year-old son, Little Chuan, to talk to. The child was eager to talk and he liked me. We became friends by

the time I had been there half a day. Little Chuan leaned against my legs and pointed at the land outside.
"My ma says the crops in the fields will be ours from
now on."

"Right, they will be your own," I answered positively
taking his thin little wrist in my hand.

"Then we will be able to eat white flour dumplings
at New Year."

"The wheat hasn't been sown yet. Wait till next
year. You'll have white dumplings next New Year."

The child was happy. His mother, who was cooking
maize gruel, turned to glance at me with a smile. But
she still said nothing.

I made several calls the following afternoon. When
I came back at night, Laichuan and his father were
snoring in the outer room. Little Chuan, sleeping beside
his mother on the bed in the inner room, was breathing evenly. Laichuan's wife did not stir. She seemed
only half asleep. Not wanting to disturb them I kept my
puttees on, simply lying down and pulling a quilt over
me.

"You aren't asleep, are you, comrade?" Laichuan's
wife asked softly, edging nearer to me. "Tell me, if we
share out the landlord's land, what about the deeds?"

This was probably a question she had considered for
a long time. I quickly told her that the old land deeds,
having been issued by the reactionary government,
didn't count. I said they could burn them in the fire.
The people's government would issue new ones.

"Good!" A great load seemed to be lifted from her
mind. She let out a long breath and was silent again.
She was so still that she might have been asleep. But I
could sense that she was still awake, probably deep in

thought, her eyes wide open. Sure enough after some time she asked again:

"Aren't you homesick, comrade?"

"If everyone stays at home who's going to fight against the reactionaries? And how can the poor people start a new life?"

"Right." Another of her doubts was resolved. She was silent again after that remark. I could see that this woman was no fool. My interest in her grew. So I inquired, "Sister-in-law, what's your name?"

For an answer she laughed softly in her quilt. "I've never been to school," she said after a while, "so I have no formal name."

"What did they call you at home?"

"An awful name. I was the last child born, so my mother called me Shoulizi which means that's all."

I told Old Ma about Shoulizi the next day. He wanted me to tell her more about women's liberation. But that day I was busy. Hurrying around until nearly noon I got the art troupe over, and arranged for a performance on a village threshing ground. At the sound of our gongs, drums, fiddles and singing, the children came flocking. Men and women hurried from their homes. People began to laugh and applaud. The silence like a stagnant pool which had prevailed in the village was completely shattered. The black lacquer gate of the despotic landlord, One-eyed Wolf, opened a slit, then immediately closed again tight. Between the acts, we did propaganda on the current situation. Some of the audience drew nearer, but others, after first edging nearer, walked away. Only the children stayed close and stood up front all through the performance. Lai-chuan, walking through the crowd, brought us two

buckets of tea. This reminded me of Shoulizi. Failing
to find her in the crowd, I ran back during an interval.
She was sitting primly on the brick bed with legs folded under her just like the day before, her head bent
over a pair of shoes she was making while she listened
to the attractive singing and the applause.

"Why don't you go to watch the fun, Shoulizi?" I
asked.

She raised her head and smiled for an answer. Sitting
down on the edge of the bed I pressed her for an explanation. "Is it proper?" she asked with a smile.

"Why not? . . ." I was on the point of giving her a
long lecture when she interrupted me with a smile, "Do
you think it's honourable to sing?"

"Sure." I was quite positive.

"Then you sing a song for me."

I hadn't suspected she could be so mischievous.
Smiling, she took my arm and asked:

"Last night you said we can burn all the landlord's
deeds. What if he puts them away?"

"Puts them away? We'll find them wherever he hides
them!"

"He's put two big bundles wrapped in cloth in the
haystack behind the temple. Can you find them?" She
continued to smile at me.

I suddenly felt that this Shoulizi, quiet and somewhat
feudal-minded, showed a real interest in land reform.
She was concerned about the land deeds and the landlord's movable property. Even more important was
that she seemed not the least bit afraid of the reactionary powers. Here was a real gem for land reform work.
I was excited. Catching hold of her arm I asked:

"Do you dare to share out the landlords' land?"

Quiet as ever, she laughed. "I have no say about that."

Singing voices and the sound of laughter drifted into the room. A little angry but very much drawn to Shoulizi who sat so primly on the brick bed, I said: "Men and women are on the same footing now, sister-in-law." I wanted to say more about the liberation of women but the applause outside told me that the next act was about to start. Being in charge of costumes, I had to hurry out.

I was supposed to be on sentry duty until midnight that night. But Old Ma, wrapped in a lined quilt, came to relieve me when I had burned only one time-measuring incense stick. Back at the cottage, I found Laichuan and his father asleep and snoring. Shoulizi had not yet gone to bed. She was twining thread beside a lamp. Happily she beckoned and made me sit beside her. Feeling my clothes, she asked whether I was cold or tired. Then she dug out a cob of corn, baked in the wrapper, from the stove. She placed it in front of me and watched me eat. Very hungry, I thought it delicious. She laughed and said:

"If we really share out the land here, we'll feed you much better than this."

"Sister-in-law!" I could not quite decide how to address her. Sometimes I felt that she was an ordinary village woman whom I could only call sister-in-law, in the old-fashioned country manner. Yet I often found her as close as a comrade, so I called her directly by name. Now she was being motherly to me. A little moved I said, "Of course the land will really be shared out. Chairman Mao says so."

"Has Chairman Mao said it? Then it's as good as

true." She became excited too but her voice dropped to a lower tone.

"As good as true."

"What if the people here don't act of one mind?"

"They will. We'll gradually educate them. Tomorrow we'll hold a meeting to unite the poor."

She stared intently at the lamp and slowly said, "That's fine." She started preparing for bed. I felt that she wanted land badly and would make a good activist. The only thing was she stubbornly believed that women were inferior to men. This was not good. So I questioned her further.

"When the land is divided, if a man is given three *mu* do you know how much a woman will get?"

"Didn't you say men and women are equal? If a man gets three, so will a woman!"

"Since you know this, you ought to come out and speak, take a hand in things."

"You want me to speak? What can I say? People would die laughing." Hiding her head in the quilt she could not help laughing herself.

I was very tired that day so I blew out the lamp and lay down to sleep. After a while she again whispered in my ear:

"Listen, it doesn't matter if the landlord hides his deeds. Since our government is in control here, the deeds don't mean anything in his hands. If the reactionaries come we won't be able to lead a good life anyway, and he'll still be rich whether he has the deeds or not. Isn't that right?"

"Yes, quite right." I couldn't help praising her. She had indeed thought things out thoroughly. The trouble was she kept it all to herself, not daring to open her mouth and speak out. Ah, Shoulizi. . . .

I was suddenly awakened from my dreams by an exclamation. "What do you know!" It was Laichuan's hoarse voice. I sat up and looked into the other room. Shoulizi was pounding garlic on the stove while close by Laichuan was shouting and brandishing a fire poker. It was already day.

"Can't you lower your voice?" said she, without so much as raising her eyelids.

"A mere woman and you have learned to be so meddlesome. Dividing the land, and sharing out the land. Is that the kind of thing for you women to talk about?" Laichuan now spoke in a lower tone but he was still making her feel his weight.

"Why not? I'll end up like my mother at the very worst." Shoulizi spoke out!

I lay down softly again for fear of interrupting their argument. But Laichuan had seen me. He swallowed what he wanted to say and stalked out with two water buckets.

That day I told Old Ma the episode. He was silent for quite a while before he said with a sigh, "That's why we say land reform is digging up the old roots of feudal power. When the roots are shaken, other things will have to stir."

The solidarity meeting of the poor peasants and hired hands was held the next day in Laichuan's house. More than twenty paupers, faces pale and backs bent from the oppression and exploitation of landlords and reactionaries, crept one by one into Laichuan's house after dark. Shoulizi came out to add oil and to put two more wicks in the lamp. Then she disappeared into the inner room, and let down the door curtain.

When the meeting started Laichuan talked briefly about uniting to fight against the landlords. There was a pause after he finished. Nobody would open his mouth. He waited for some time, then got angry by the sight of everyone merely smoking and coughing. Getting red in the neck, he suddenly pounded the table.

"Those who want land, stay!" he shouted in a hoarse voice. "Come what may, we'll see it through. Those who don't can get out!" This outburst not only startled the people who came to the meeting, even I and Old Ma were stunned. One timid individual got to his feet tremblingly: "Laichuan. . . . You know me, I. . . ." He wanted to leave. A few more stood up. The meeting, which had taken four days to prepare, was on the point of being broken up by Laichuan's shouting. Quickly Old Ma rose. But before he could say anything, the door curtain was lifted. With downcast eyes, Shoulizi stood in the doorway.

"Villagers," she said, timid and shy, "I'd say we want land!"

This softly uttered sentence was even more of a surprise to everyone than Laichuan's outburst. Those who had stood up and were about to leave paused. Though her lips trembled slightly, Shoulizi spoke steadily and clearly:

"Our fathers and generations before them never asked to share out the landlord's land, but they never had a decent life either. You all know how the landlord killed my mother and threw her body to the dogs. So I say, let's divide the land and fight for a way to live." She raised her eyes only after she had finished, quickly swept the room with a glance, then vanished again. There was utter silence, no one made a move. Laichuan, mouth agape, seemed also to have been calmed by his wife's speech. He stood up abruptly after a while, tightened his belt and cried hoarsely. "Villagers, there's no way out for us unless we divide up the land. We'll pledge with blood to unite tightly together and divide the damned land."

At these passionate words of his, the atmosphere in the little room became animated. Two young men stood up and spoke enthusiastically. A grey-bearded old man walked forward with a squawking rooster in one hand and a chopper in another, to make a pledge in blood.

After the meeting we organized a home guard and posted sentries to watch One-eyed Wolf, the despotic landlord. Yanzhuang had awakened. The people no longer hugged the walls as they walked. The village resounded with laughter and singing. With both hands they lifted the big mountain which had been weighing them down for thousands of years, and smashed it to smithereens.

As we were measuring out the land and driving in the landmarks for the new owners, Laichuan, holding his son, Little Chuan, joyfully turned somersaults on the land he had been allotted. Shoulizi could not help smiling though there were tears in her eyes. How I hated to leave these people who had finally begun a new life. But we had to go.

Muffled artillery boomed in the south on the day of our departure. Shoulizi helped me spread my bed cover, fold my quilt and roll up my bedding. Silently, she helped to put the pack on my back. Little Chuan hung around me refusing to let me out of his sight. I told

Shoulizi that she must be braver in the future, she should speak up and do some community work too, not hide herself at home any more. She promised compliantly, eager to assure me. Putting a stack of *kaoliang* pancakes she had prepared into my hands she said: "When the wheat is in next year, I'll mill the flour and have it waiting for you."

"We're sure to come, Shoulizi. Perhaps before the wheat is in, perhaps after. Maybe we'll see you every day. We're sure to win."

The people now had land but they still needed guns. With the permission of our superiors, Old Ma left his rifle with the villagers of Yanzhuang. Then we said goodbye to Laichuan and his family.

Our troops were on the march every day, sometimes fifty *li*, sometimes seventy. Large tracts of land stretched endlessly beneath our feet. The crops in the field, ripening, turned a dark gold. A few months later we were marching past black tracts of earth, gleaming and bare. Then wheat seeds were dropped on the vast land, wheat seeds with the power to push through mountains, afraid neither of the bitter cold nor wind and frost. The wheat germinated and sprouted, carpeting the black earth with tender green. In the spring of 1948, when the wheat was only half a foot high and before Shoulizi could mill that wheat flour she promised to keep for me, I visited Yanzhuang a second time.

To trap and destroy an enemy contingent, our troops lured them into an encirclement. We wiped them out east of Yanzhuang. After the battle, as usual, our unit stopped for a day or two to rest and regroup. I remembered Yanzhuang and asked for half a day's leave.

It was already dark by the time I hurried down to

the village. A strong smell of burnt cloth accosted me before I even entered Yanzhuang. My heart began to pound. Was it possible that the enemy we had just annihilated east of here had passed through on their way?

What had happened to the village? And Shoulizi? That gun of Old Ma, had they buried it or was it still slung over the shoulder of a Yanzhuang villager? Bending slightly, I started to run towards the village.

"You there, halt!" With a shout, someone burst out of the darkness. His voice and his accent warmed my heart; someone from Yanzhuang was standing guard. Once emancipated, they would never let history turn backwards, they would never let the old days come again.

"Old uncle," I cried, very much moved as I ran up to him. "It's me. It's me."

"Will you halt now!" With a click he pushed in the bolt. How I longed to rush up to the old man and hug him, but I had to obey his order. The old man with the gun came closer. I recognized him immediately in the starlight. He was Laichuan's father, that silent old man who kept a pipe clamped between his teeth all day. During the land reform he had never uttered a single sentence, but whenever there was a meeting, he was always there. It didn't matter whether it was a quick get-together meeting of the leaders or a discussion among the activists. He always came and listened whether he had been invited or not. Of course I never paid much attention to him, nor did I remember to ask him what he thought or whether he had anything to say. Now he was a sentry, gun in hand and looking serious. Laichuan's father was a Yanzhuang sentry. In a stirred voice I addressed him by name. Taken aback, he moved closer to stare at me. When at last he recognized me, he tucked the gun under one arm, rushed up, gripped both of my hands in his large calloused ones and shook them again and again. "How we've longed for your return. . . ." he said with a sob.

"You've had a hard time, uncle."

"It's not the hardships." With one hand he brushed away a tear while the other hand kept its hold on mine.

"Where are Laichuan and the others?" I felt a little apprehensive to see him doing sentry duty.

"Laichuan took the other young men of the village off to work at the front."

"Ah!" I was reassured to learn that they were safe.

"And sister-in-law?" I asked.

"You mean Little Chuan's ma. . . . She's here." For some reason he choked over the sentence.

I was eager to go and see Shoulizi so I hurriedly bade the conscientious sentry goodbye. Before long at a crossroad I saw an old man pass by with a woman in custody. Since they and I were all in a hurry I didn't stop to make inquiries. But I recognized the woman as the wife of One-eyed Wolf, a despotic landlord now dead. By the light of the stars, I could see that a good number of the villagers' thatched cottages were gone. What was left were only broken sections of scorched mud walls and smashed crockery and torn cotton padding littering the ground on all sides. However, the charred rafters and beams had already been piled up, and the open ground was covered with stacks of mud bricks. In the hazy starlight the village appeared quiet and stern.

I found Shoulizi in a thatched shed which had been

put up in one corner of the yard where Laichuan's house had stood. She was slightly thinner and more sunburnt, and her eyes appeared even larger. Seated on a thin layer of wheat stalks, head bent, she was quietly mending a flour sieve, slowly weaving a fine and meticulous web over the holes with fine horsehair. It was as if she were still sitting on her own warm brick bed at home and the enemy had never been here, as if this low thatched shed, this pallet of wheat straw and the broken walls outside did not exist at all. Dear Shoulizi, didn't you see what happened, or were you really untouched by it all? There you sat so quietly with bent head, getting implements ready for the wheat harvest.

Happening to look up, she discovered me. Her face registered no surprise, she only smiled. However, in contrast to her usual quiet and calm manner, she stood up and began bustling about. She lifted the lid off the pot, picked up the water ladle, gathered a bunch of hay and unwrapped a package. After all this bustling, she brought me a bowl of hot water. Now she quieted down, resuming her ordinary calm and composure as she took my hands and sat down by my side. I asked her how she managed when the enemy was here.

"Stayed out in the wilds," she answered simply.

"What about Laichuan?"

"Him? He took our home guards, shouldered that gun and went round and round, firing one shot here and another there." She smiled at this point, probably at the recollection of the effect of those occasional shots. Noticing that she was alone in the shed, I asked, "Where's Little Chuan?"

Shoulizi avoided my inquiring glance. "You know," she began after a pause, "Little Chuan was so happy

when we were given a share of land. After the wheat
was sown he kept going down to the field for a look.
He was counting on white wheat flour dumplings for
New Year. You remember that the piece of land we
got was close by the village. When the enemy came we
went out to hide in the wilds. We were cold and hungry.
The child's mind, however, was on the wheat field.
'Ma,' he said, 'will the reactionaries dig out our wheat
seeds?' 'They won't be able to dig out all the seeds,'
I assured him. 'What if the landlord takes back our
land?' he asked. I told him that the land couldn't be
moved but still he wasn't reassured.

" 'Ma, I'm small, let me steal back for a peep,' he
pleaded. Do you think I'd let him go? The reactionaries had been in the village only two days and the wife
of One-eyed Wolf was acting high and mighty. She
invited the Kuomintang officers to her house and they
talked of collecting back rents from the villagers, of
killing and burning. How could I let Little Chuan go
back to the village? The trouble was at midnight I
fell asleep and the child ran back. . . ." Shoulizi
stopped to poke at the wick in the oil lamp and to
calm her own emotions. I recalled the landlord's wife
I had seen on my way — still wearing an expensive
black silk padded jacket. I ground my teeth with wrath.
Just then, the straw door curtain was lifted and an
old man entered. "Laichuan's wife, that woman wants
a drink of water. Should I let her have some?"

"No!" I cried. I felt the old man needn't have asked
such a question.

"Better give her some, grandad, let her live to see
us in control here." Shoulizi told the old man calmly,
very much like a commander. The old man agreed and

went off convinced. Shoulizi turned back to continue our chat. I watched her closely. She seemed no different from the old Shoulizi. With her eyes on the lamp, she told me slowly what had happened, speaking so clearly and in such detail that I felt I had shared the experience with her.

When Shoulizi could not find her son she knew where the child had gone and she realized that he would not be back. She neither wept nor wailed but sat there in a daze. As Laichuan was away with the other home guards, the folks were worried that bottling up her feelings like that she'd make herself ill. They advised her to have a good cry, but she shook her head without a word, her eyes dry. It was not until the sun had sunk to the top of the mountain that she told the others: "I'll slip back quietly for a look. One look, that's all I want." She left there and then. No one could stop her. Afraid that she would come to harm, the villagers sent someone to fetch Laichuan.

The sun was setting. Night, so dreaded by the Chiang Kai-shek army, was descending. Shoulizi scrambled up the mud hill at the west end of the village. Yanzhuang, scorched and black, was still smoking. Burnt gateways, licked by the tongue of the fire, gaped like so many black mouths. A couple of Kuomintang sentries, their heads low, arms cradling their rifles, kicked at the pillows and chopsticks littering the ground and stamped on broken crockery and dried peppers. Wind dogged their footsteps, swirling up the ashes and whistling through the trees. . . .

"Where is Little Chuan?" It suddenly dawned on Shoulizi that it was not enough just to drive the reactionaries out of the village. Wherever they went they would repeat what they did at Yanzhuang. The enemy must be cleanly and thoroughly wiped out, not just driven away. For a moment Shoulizi forgot Little Chuan and the sharp pain that only a mother knows. Lying flat on the hill-side, she saw everything, imprinting the memory deep in her heart. Then she spied her husband crawling to her from the side. His face was ashen and he panted heavily. Without a word, he took her around to the east of the village to a small pine grove behind One-eyed Wolf's house. No sooner had she crouched down behind a tree than a child's voice reached her ears from the threshing ground in front of the house. "No. No, I won't kneel." It was her Little Chuan. Shoulizi's whole heart quivered. She snatched the gun out of her husband's hands. . . .

Could she let what happened twenty years ago repeat itself? The fate suffered by the mother must not befall the son! When Shoulizi was nine her father had left home to seek work. It was on this same piece of ground that the landlord forced her mother to kneel all night on two pieces of tiles, facing towards the north and holding up two pieces of bricks. Her crime was inability to pay the rent. Shoulizi had stayed beside her mother, weeping through the bitter winter night. The next morning her mother's face was covered by a layer of frost. She could no longer persevere, and breathed her last on this same threshing ground. All night through, mother had repeated only three words in Shoulizi's ear: "Do not forget."

The gun Old Ma had left went off with a bang. Not knowing the source of the shot, the enemy was thrown into confusion. Her hands trembling, Shoulizi stood erect in front of the pinewoods, the gun in her hands. She felt a certain satisfaction, though she had not hit a single enemy. Laichuan pulled her into the woods and taking up the gun fired a shot into the midst of the enemy before he turned to flee with her. But his wife pulled away. She ran forward a little for a last look at Little Chuan. The child lay in a pool of blood, quietly staring into the boundless sky. Enemy soldiers milled round yelling and crying, guns barked and bullets whistled through the air. Her son had died, refusing to yield to the enemy. Shoulizi turned round and dashed off. She was not running away but simply going at high speed towards a certain target, she was running towards a target she had chosen. Yanzhuang was no longer silent.

Shoulizi poked at the oil lamp till it burned brighter. Carefully wiping the drop of oil that had spattered on to her finger on her jet black hair, she said, "I never knew that a gun is so good, so important."

"Now that you've caught the she-wolf, what do you intend to do with her?"

Shoulizi looked at me and then she said, pronouncing the words one by one distinctly, "Do with her? We've got the Party's policy to go by. We shan't beat her or curse her. We just want her to watch us build our new homes, watch us eat and drink well. Then we'll have her taken to the district for a public trial."

Was it necessary to console her with words? In her, I felt only a firm confidence and strength which would quickly bring whole rows of new houses and abundant grain. It would speed the arrival of victory. I became impatient too. I wanted to rush back to my unit to do all the work I was able. Just then, the old man who had come before reappeared.

"Laichuan's wife, we've gathered together what wood there's left out of the ruins. It seems practically every family is short of timber for their house beams."

Shoulizi considered the problem silently. Instead of hurrying her for a reply, the old man fished out his pipe, squatted down to smoke in a corner and patiently waited for her to deliberate the matter.

"I think, grandad, those who have trees can use their own, those without any should get timber from the pinewoods behind the One-eyed Wolf's house. Is that all right?"

"Sure," said the old man, again convinced that she was right and turning to leave.

"I'll go with you," Shoulizi said on second thought. "Let's talk it over with the folks and see."

"Why bother? This is the right way." Grandad didn't think any more talk was necessary.

Shoulizi stood up. She seemed to have forgotten my presence completely until she reached the door. "Let's continue our talk later," she said turning round. "But you must not go yet." She went out of the thatched shed quickly and disappeared in the darkness.

The shed was very low. Half-reclining against the pallet, I stared at the dark night outside through a crack in the mat door curtain. I could not picture Shoulizi talking things over with the folks and distributing the wood among them. When I closed my eyes, it was the old Shoulizi who appeared; she sat primly on the brick bed, saying with a smile, "Is it proper?" Quickly though, this image receded. In its place, appeared a woman with a sunburnt face whose movements were quick and sure. As she stood in the pinewoods, big trees fell at her feet and she solemnly told One-eyed

Wolf's wife: "You just watch. Watch us build new homes, watch us eat and drink well, watch us, the people, rule the country."

... The lamplight blurred. Time flew past with a whirr of golden wings. I fell asleep.

Wakened by smoke choking me, I opened my eyes to discover that someone had put a quilt over me. The thatched shed was shrouded in smoke and steam. Shoulizi sat by the stove at the door feeding the fire. Veiled by wisps of white smoke, her face seemed softer and more serene in the flickering firelight, not nearly as militant as the face of the Shoulizi in my dream.

"It's not yet midnight. Sleep a little more," she said when she saw me pushing away the quilt.

"It's about time. Have you finished your business?"

Shoulizi sighed. "With Laichuan and the home guards gone we have to build our homes and protect them at the same time. It's a heavy responsibility."

The home guards had gone to help the PLA at the front. Those left behind had shouldered the task of guarding the community interests. The masters of Yanzhuang now had strength enough to go beyond their own homes. They were pushing history forward.

"The responsibility may be heavy, but you people are doing pretty well."

"What do you mean pretty well?" Shoulizi turned her head to take in the things round her with a glance. "If we manage to get all the cottages built before wheat harvest, it'll really be good." Her voice was full of gladness though there was no smile on her face.

Well, I'd seen what I had wanted to see and could feel reassured about the folks I'd been anxious about.

The night air was chilly. It must have been past midnight. I stood up and adjusted my puttees. I had to go.

"Wait a second!" Shoulizi got up. She lifted the lid of the pot, letting out a jet of steam which rose to the ceiling. The pot was half filled with boiling water. In the top half slabbed against the sides of the pot were six flatcakes of red *kaoliang* flour. She filled my canteen with boiled water, wrapped the flatcakes in a piece of cloth and put them in my hands. "I made the cakes for you to eat on the way."

"Why have you done that, Shoulizi?" I could see there was wild grass gruel in an earthen bowl but here she was giving me good *kaoliang* flour. It made me a little angry with her.

"We'll be all right as soon as we harvest the wheat. . . ." Shoulizi dropped her eyes. "I do want to give you something good now. . . ."

"When the wheat's harvested, I'll come again and you can give me something good." I put the flatcakes back in her hands and picked up the hot canteen. I turned to leave, knowing that she would feel bad. But what else could I do? After a few steps I noticed that she had not come out with me. She stood where she was with a wooden look, the package of cakes in her hands. The sight made me uneasy. "Shoulizi," I turned round to say, "I'll be coming back in a couple of months. Will you have white flour milled and waiting for me?"

"I'll send it to you." This said in a tone that seemed to end the question, she remained motionless. I had to leave now. After I had gone some distance, I looked back. She was leaning against the door of the thatched shed, the steaming cakes still in her hands. With the faint light of the lamp behind her she seemed bigger in stature. Somewhere from the village came the clop, clop of wood being chopped; the villagers of Yanzhuang were making their beams.

I went further and further away from Yanzhuang but I felt that along with victory, Shoulizi was close behind me. She was there behind every fighter, that package of steaming flatcakes in her hands, her sunburnt face serene and resolute. When we reached camp after a march and when we came back from the front lines for a short pause, late at night or early in the morning, as soon as we knocked lightly at a villager's door she would appear promptly to unbolt and open it. When we were tired and hungry there was always warm water for our feet and piping hot potato soup or millet gruel. When we set out again, the narrow long ration bags slung over our shoulders would contain the pre-cooked wheat flour or dried slices of steamed bread she had made for us. When we felt hot and parched on our march, she appeared with buckets of cold tea. Sometimes she silently slipped a couple of warm boiled eggs into our pockets, at times it was a handful of red dates. Our feet were shod in shoes she had stitched and stockings she had made. Into our ears she poured only one request: "Wipe out the reactionaries' god-damned army and defend our good life."

Snow swirled silently and stealthily. An old worm-eaten tree close by squeaking under the weight of the snow finally collapsed with a crash. Lamplights flashed in villages near and far. Here and there sparks floated from cottage chimneys. The people and the army along the Huaihai front were happily spending the last few hours of 1948.

In my mind I saw Yanzhuang lying like the villages near by: Snow covered the wide land but people were living in newly built cottages, celebrating the New Year. And Shoulizi? She . . . perhaps she was sitting with legs folded under her on the warm brick bed. . . . It was still snowing, the snowflakes falling thicker and thicker. The row of footprints on the road was quickly covered by a layer of new snow. I tried to imagine how Shoulizi looked now.

There was the cracking of whips down the road as a team of carts appeared. The carters seemed to be all women. Their shrill voices calling to the animals reached my ears before the carts were near enough for me to see them clearly. The woman in the lead was of medium height; her hair and mouth were muffled under a big cloth shawl. I spied a pair of fine wide eyes. She strode along, holding her horse's bridle.

This road led to the front line region a bit further down. Where did they think they were taking the carts?

"What have you got on those carts, comrades?" I stopped them. The one in front called to the animals to a halt and eyed me from head to toe.

"Grain," she replied.

"Do you know where you'll be if you go any further? Where are you taking your grain?"

"We don't know. We're just following our team leader." By then the other carters had come close enough to answer.

"And who's the team leader?" My eyes rested on the one with the fine eyes leading the line of carts. She smiled.

"I'm not the team leader. There," she said, indicating the footprints in the snow with her chin. "Our team leader has gone ahead to make contact. We are following her footprints, we can't go wrong." The clever young woman answered distinctly and quite steadily. For some reason, her attitude made me imagine things and this fancy made me feel closer to them.

"But how dangerous it is for you to go on this way! Suppose your leader blunders into the enemy?"

The women carters were at first taken aback but immediately the one with the fine eyes burst into a chuckle. Turning to her mates she said, "Our leader blunder into the enemy?"

A burst of laughter greeted her words. I was the object of their laughter and they were quite merciless in their mirth.

"Our team leader went to the front when our army was fighting at Nianzhuang and at Jinan. D'you think she'd get lost and blunder into the enemy!" One of the carters said this with pride. Apparently they had a capable team leader whose prestige was very high.

"No matter what you say, comrades, your carts had better not go any further," I continued patiently.

"Can't be done. Without our team leader's orders, we can't stop." Fine Eyes cracked her whip as she talked and made ready to go. At that moment a stream of dazzling flares sprang into the air. The next moment the trees and their shadows were quivering all round us. Big snowflakes danced like so many white butterflies in the strong glare against a background of silvery white. The dozen or so women carters stood out vividly before my eyes, militant and brave. Some wore their hair in a bun at the nape of the neck, others plaited their hair into a big braid which hung down their backs. All of them wore the same leather belts round their padded gowns with a water ladle at the waist. The flares did not arouse their attention much as they returned to the carts in their charge and got ready to go on. I scrutinized their faces one by one feeling for some reason that I might find that familiar face among them. It was a crazy idea of course. They filed past, hands on the bridles, walking close beside their carts, trailing the footprints their team leader had left behind.

"Hey, comrades, what's your team leader's name?" Suddenly I felt an urgent desire to know the name of this team leader.

"Yan Zhengying." Their answer came back to me from a distance away.

"Yan Zhengying!" I couldn't say whether I was glad or disappointed. "Why isn't it Shoulizi?"

Back in my billet I found on my rucksack a wooden bowl full of newly fried beans. This must be the doing of Big Dragon, the son of my host. I had heard him coaxing his mother for fried beans in the morning, besides, he'd already told me he'd treat me to beans.

I placed the beans by my pillow and blew out the lamp.

I was wakened by voices and muffled laughter in the middle of the night. Opening my eyes, I found that the women carters I met on the way had arrived. They were warming themselves round the fire and talking in low tones evidently trying not to wake me. As I appreciated their consideration, I lay quietly pretending to still be asleep.

"It's all very well to say take our grain to the front

lines. We haven't even heard a single shot. Call that sending grain to the front line?" This was the girl with the fine wide eyes. Judging by her tone she meant to take the grain right into the trenches before she'd feel satisfied.

"Weren't we told to take it to the Rear-line Services and Supply? Naturally that must be a bit behind the front line."

"Who says? Didn't our team leader say before the soldiers and horses make a move the grain and fodder must arrive first? We must get there even before the Liberation Army."

Gradually, they forgot about the person who was supposed to be sleeping.

"Can you guess why Erman is so anxious to get closer to the front line?" A new question was posed by the woman sitting beside my bed. Both those who wanted to send the grain to the front and those who were satisfied with sending it to Rear-line Services and Supply crowded up to ask, "Why?"

"To look for someone."

"Ha, ha. . . ." The sound of their merriment nearly burst through the roof.

"Ha, ha . . . why do you turn back in the end?" I was just going to join in their merriment when suddenly the door opened. Behind the rush of cold air and snow into the room a woman entered. Was it my imagination or was she real? Yes, it was Shoulizi. She wore a man's long padded gown, with the front tucked up under her sash. Her head was wrapped in a towel. Standing in the doorway, her cheeks crimson from the cold, she said, "Sisters, our animals have been fed and we've warmed up. Let's go."

"Shoulizi!" I bolted from the bed.

"Oh!" She walked up to my bed, recognized me and was overwhelmed. Her hands gripped mine tightly.

"Is everything all right at Yanzhuang?" I didn't know where to begin.

"Yes, yes, everything's fine. The wheat harvest was excellent last summer and the autumn crops were pretty good. Laichuan joined the army last spring."

"So you know our team leader," cried the merry women carters, surprised and delighted, crowding round our shoulders.

"Look at her, is she the kind to blunder into the enemy?" Fine Eyes glanced at her team leader with pride. Still remembering our conversation on the road, she was challenging me.

"No, she's not that kind." I looked at Shoulizi and saw in my mind's eye the woman who sat on the brick bed with her legs folded under her.

"Why have you changed your name?"

"When I was admitted into the Communist Party the Party branch gave me this name." Shoulizi talked in the same old quiet and shy manner.

It was she who had gone to the front lines when we were fighting in Nianzhuang and at Jinan. It was she who went where the shells and bullets flew. I remembered how she sat on the ground amid the rubble quietly mending a flour sieve with horse-hair. Yes, it was she, this same Shoulizi. As a matter of fact I had no trouble imagining her there.

"And the cottages? Have they all been put up?" These weren't the things I wanted to talk about but it was what I said.

"Yes, we've rebuilt all the cottages long ago. One-eyed Wolf's wife was given a public trial. . . ." The woman who had sat beside my bed didn't give Shoulizi a chance to finish but cut in to say, "Look, our team leader's met an old friend. Why, oh, why can't our little sister Erman there find the one she's been looking for?"

"Ha, ha. . . ." The laughter that followed was so loud and merry that the horses outside started to neigh in alarm. "It's getting late," said Shoulizi getting to her feet. "When our carts reach their destination and we've finished our job, I'll come back to see you." With that she took her carters away leaving the room like a gust of wind. The next instant, the clear cracking of whips sounded outside, and in a rumble of wheels and the snorting of the horses, they left.

How silly of me! Was there any need for me to go for a look? Since things were all right at Yanzhuang and the people were all right, naturally new cottages had been built and crops planted in the fields. The crops were growing and so were the people. All this was as plain as day. Was there any need to make a third visit to Yanzhuang?

Pale white light began to show on the eastern horizon. Enemy transport planes were droning again, probably attempting an air drop in spite of the snow. But failing to locate their target when snow covered everything, they merely whined sadly overhead. I threw a coat over my shoulders and went outside. Deep cart tracks and footprints in the snow formed straggly trails, all leading south.

December 1960
Translated by Qin Sheng

Just a Happy-Go-Lucky Girl

THE birds were silent, and the cock hadn't yet crowed when I stirred. The sky was still dark as I waited for the noise that was supposed to awake me. The old Party secretary should have told me what to expect instead of leaving me guessing.

I had arrived at this village at dusk the previous day. Having met the old Party secretary and arranged my lodgings, I went to the canteen where they were already washing up, but they heated up some porridge for me. I took it for granted that there would be no more dishes and that I'd have to make do with a peppery sauce, when to my surprise a plate of fresh broad beans was pushed at me through a window. The girl disappeared before I could thank her, but I caught a glimpse of her long plaits tied with green ribbons.

When the old Party secretary later came over to have a chat, I asked him about the girl who had given me the beans. He laughed, "Ah! It must be her!"

Her? Who was she?

"She's a treasure. You'll see her tomorrow morning. She'll wake you up."

How interesting! But I had awoke before then and spoilt the surprise. As dawn drew near, many noises were heard. Doors creaking, people coughing, the footsteps of those going out for breakfast or to fetch water, oxen lowing, water running into the seed beds. . . .

These faint noises, magnified in the clear morning air, make me wonder which was supposed to be the one to wake me.

It was soon daylight. The birds chirped and the cock crowed. Many doors opened. A flock of ducks went quacking down to the river. How could I lie there waiting? Rising, I heard someone apparently stumble down the wooden stairs next door. Then a girl's voice cried, "Bye, mum!" A door banged and she began singing loudly.

"It's her!" I realized. I pushed open the window and saw a girl with a satchel walking away, her two long plaits swinging behind her.

"Hey there!" I called to her. She stopped and walked back to my window. Pointing at me she said, "I knew you were coming. Your name is Ru, isn't it?"

"And yours is Treasure."

She blinked, smiled and said, "I'm Ashu."

She was quite a tall girl, with a full baby-face. "How old are you?" I asked.

"Fourteen."

"What grade are you in?"

She seemed embarrassed and replied hesitantly, "The sixth grade." Then she added, "I started school rather late."

With a cheeky smile she pleaded, "Tell me a story this evening. I'm sure you know many."

"How do you know?" She seemed an interesting girl. I put out my arm to catch hold of her but she dodged away. As she ran away she called back, "A little bird told me!"

I leaned on the sill inhaling the fresh cool air. The sky was a pale blue tinged with pink. The green rice seedlings rippled in the breeze, tender and sweet like young Ashu.

The bell rang, marking the start of a new work day. This year the harvest here was rather poor. At first the ears of wheat had been full, but just as the wheat was turning yellow, it rained several times. Afraid that the wheat would rot in the fields, the old Party secretary had ordered the villagers to harvest it. As the crop wasn't fully ripe, they had a hundred catties less per *mu* than the other villages. Thus the villagers received less income and the state suffered a loss. The old Party secretary and Ashu's mother, who was in charge of production, felt very upset, especially the old man who held himself responsible. At noon, the three of us met briefly in the kitchen of Ashu's home where they briefed me on the situation and discussed work. Ashu sat doing her homework in the sitting-room.

Ashu's mother began, "This summer we had a poor harvest."

"We must make up for it," said the old Party secretary. From the sitting-room Ashu was heard reading aloud, ". . . After the Sino-Japanese War in 1894, the imperialist countries increased their aggression against China. In order to. . . ."

"What shall we do?" Ashu's mother asked again.

His voice emotional, the old Party secretary said, "We'll have to make up the difference with the rice and cotton crops."

"Uncle," Ashu called, "to whom did the concessions belong in the past?"

"Why, to the imperialists of course!" the old man answered her slowly. But her mother grumbled,

"Haven't we enough worries without being bothered by your questions? You young people are so carefree."

"That's not true. My worries are right here," she retorted patting her textbook.

"She'll be sitting her graduation exams soon," said the old Party secretary. "Why worry her about other things?" Returning to the subject of production, he continued, "We'll divide our work force so that one half collects the fertilizer while the other transplants the rice seedlings."

"But there's only one fertilizer boat," Ashu's mother interjected. "What shall we do?"

". . . In order to establish factories and build railways in China, the imperialists grabbed the concessions and divided up China into their spheres of influence." Ashu was concentrating on her history.

"A little quieter please, Ashu. We're discussing something important here." Her mother's voice called sharply.

Glancing reprovingly at her, the old Party secretary said, "It's our fault. Don't take it out on the child." Then, producing a key from his pocket, he called, "Go and study in my room, Ashu."

He lived alone, since his wife had died many years earlier and his children all worked away from home. Many times they had asked him to go and live with them, afraid he was too lonely, but he always refused, saying, "I'm far too busy to be lonely."

Ashu came into the room looking serious, her book in her hand. As she took the key, she made a face at me.

Everybody loved her. When her mother scolded her,

the old Party secretary would humour her. But he told me Ashu never took advantage of her popularity.

By night, my mind was full of rice seedlings, fertilizer and irrigation schemes. . . . The weather was getting warmer. Although we still wore our padded winter clothes, the trees were in bud, flowers were blossoming and everywhere the ground was turning green. Nature was quickening. This was the time to transplant the rice seedlings, give them water and fertilizer and weed them. A good harvest would partly depend on what was done now. Life here was busier, harder and more significant than in some other places. I was mulling this over when Ashu interrupted me.

"Tell me a story, please," she demanded as she leaned over my shoulders. There was no getting out of it. Looking at her youthful face, I decided to tell her about the struggles of the peasants before Liberation. But she asked, "Was their life so terrible? Then I don't want to hear about it."

"What do you want to hear about then?"

"Oh, something nice and interesting."

While she wanted to hear stories with happy endings, I felt she ought to hear more than that. So from that evening on I had to tell two stories a night, one nice and one not so nice. She would listen with a solemn expression, never interrupting or laughing. Her eyes, full of wonder and happiness, gazed at me steadily until I had finished the story. Only then would she relax and laugh.

Ashu's mother came to my place every evening telling me about their work. A pig had fallen sick. More fertilizer was needed in the paddy fields. Sometimes she entered as I was halfway through a story, so that

Ashu became anxious. Then her mother would comment, "Just a happy-go-lucky girl with no worries!"

While I agreed with her, I also agreed with the old Party secretary about not burdening her with worries. Every evening after mother and daughter had gone home, each with their own thoughts, I tried to assess which of the two attitudes was more correct and always failed.

As the rice ripened, Ashu graduated from her primary school. I discovered that she not only wanted to hear nice stories, but also liked to make a game out of everything she did. The flock of ducks belonging to her mother didn't return home at dusk one day, and although her mother went down to the river to search, she couldn't find them. Tired and worried, she returned to see Ashu immersed in a story. Angrily she told her to go and look for the ducks.

"OK." Ashu said cheerfully as she took a long bamboo pole asking me to accompany her to hold her torch for her. Far from being annoyed, she seemed delighted.

It was getting dark. I walked behind, shining the torch at the trees on the river bank, the reeds in the water and all the likely hiding-places of the ducks. Yet Ashu walked straight ahead, never once looking to see where the ducks might be.

"Why don't you look for them?" I thought I should remind her.

Not bothering to look round she answered, "It's no fun that way."

So searching for ducks could be fun? Silently I followed her across a bridge until we came to a bend in the river. Here she halted beside a big tree and slowly went down the bank to the river's edge. Then she called for me to join her. Climbing down, I found her sitting in a big wooden tub used by the villagers to gather water chestnuts. Gaily she urged me to get on board. Never in my life had I sat in a wooden tub on the river, and at night too! I stiffened as the tub lurched to one side. Sitting nervously behind her, I clutched the sides tightly while Ashu, half leaning over the edge, picked water chestnuts and paddled with her hands. The long bamboo pole lay with one end across her legs and the other cutting through the splashing water.

"Lo, lo, lo!" she called to the ducks as she shelled the nuts. I ventured to let go my grip on the sides and eat too. Though the water chestnuts were small, they were tender and delicious. By the time we had eaten our fill and found the ducks, we still had plenty of water chestnuts to take home. I had to admit we'd had a lot of fun. But what if we hadn't found the ducks? When I asked her, she was surprised. "Not find them?" she said. "I thought my mother was the one who always worried."

"Sometimes it's necessary to worry a little," I explained. "You know your wheat harvest was very poor."

"Yes. I hear them talking about it every day. I was planning to buy a bike this year, but now I won't. Walking makes my legs strong and it's fun too."

"Do you really think your not buying a bike will make such a difference?" I was testing her.

She couldn't find an answer to that, so after a moment she laughed and asked, "What shall I do then?"

She was right. What could a girl of fourteen be expected to do? I smiled back.

"Lo, lo, lo!" she called to the ducks, as she climbed on to the bank. They flapped their wings splashing water everywhere.

How happy Ashu's mother was to see her daughter return with the noisy flock and the water chestnuts! But at the sight of her rolled-up trousers and bare feet, she sighed. Both Ashu and I knew what that meant, but she said nothing.

Two days later, a meeting of the Party and Youth League members and young activists was held in the commune to assess the work during the first half of the year and praise the good workers as an example to the others. Leading comrades from the county were also invited to attend. The evening before the meeting, as nothing was happening in the team, I tried to read but couldn't concentrate. I found myself making up a story for Ashu. It was strange she didn't come. Next door there was no noise in her home. I blew out my lamp and went out to look for her. At the entrance to the village, I saw her approaching, a bundle under her arm.

She seemed in high spirits and called out to me, "Are you going to the meeting tomorrow?" But without waiting for my reply, she continued, "So am I." Drawing near she told me excitedly, "I got an invitation. I'm going too." But she added softly, "I'm not a Youth League member yet."

When I asked her where she had been, she quickly put her bundle behind her back and said, "I won't tell you." Then she immediately confided, "I went to borrow a pretty blouse for the meeting."

Past a rustling gold paddy field, a lamp was moving in an experimental plot of late rice. Some people were catching moths there.

"Are there many moths?" Ashu and I called as we walked over.

"Yes! The weather has been so dry lately." The old Party secretary was making a three-legged stand over a basin. His lantern was on the ground.

"The rice crop looks good," I commented.

He looked up, the wrinkles at the corners of his eyes smoothing away. "Yes. Can you calculate the yield?" He liked to hear other people's calculations.

But Ashu interrupted, unable to contain herself any longer," Uncle, I'm going to take part in the meeting tomorrow."

"Wonderful!" he said, but his mind was on the crop.

"I'll guarantee seven hundred and fifty catties," Grandpa Tiangen said confidently.

"That's excellent!" Ashu exclaimed, adding softly to me, "Now I can buy my bike!"

Sighing, the old Party secretary said, "That's what everyone has calculated, but it's far from satisfactory." Shaking his head, he added, "We won't reach our target." He seemed to have some secret quota.

Not understanding, Ashu asked, "Which village are we challenging?"

"Which village? We're competing all the time, whether we like it or not." He rose and picked up his lantern. His long shadow fell over the paddy field. "Why can some people achieve so much in their lives while others cannot, even if they live several times over?" Gazing into the distance he seemed to be questioning himself, the night sky, the land or vast stretches of fields.

His pipe in his mouth, Grandpa Tiangen said slowly, "Some people live like a dragon, others like a worm!"

The conversation of these two old men baffled the happy girl. Why talk about the meaning of life when discussing production? Looking at both of them she asked, "What's so good about being a dragon?"

"You'll know later," the old Party secretary smiled at her fondly. Then he asked her, "Tell me, as we got ninety catties less wheat yield per *mu*, how much less did we harvest altogether from seventeen hundred *mu*?"

"Altogether one hundred and fifty-three thousand catties," Ashu calculated quickly, wondering what he was driving at.

Picking up some straw rope from the ground, the old man explained, "Don't you see? The state lost that much grain."

On our way home, Ashu sighed deeply as if having finished a hard task.

Very early the next morning, Ashu dressed for the meeting in the white linen blouse with pink flowers and a pair of white gym shoes. Her plaits were tied with green ribbons. She ran in and out three times excitedly while I was eating my breakfast. Her mother, extremely proud of her, was about to say, "Just a happy-go-lucky girl with no worries!" when Ashu dragged me by the hand out of the door.

We arrived early at the commune. People stood smoking and chatting about various topics. Smoke, noise and laughter. The meeting was buoyant. Wide-eyed with excitement, Ashu found everything interesting and strange. Then suddenly she became self-conscious. . . .

"Are your rape seeds growing well this year?"

"Yes. Not bad. . . ."

"And he's doing a fine job," said somebody, pointing at the old Party secretary. Ashu smiled, embarrassed as if she had been praised. The old man was removing his grey jacket, which he wore only on special occasions and took off as soon as he entered a place, so that it was still like new after three years. Having hung up his jacket, he turned around and answered, "Even if we harvested a thousand catties of rice per *mu,* our yield is still lower than yours."

Ashu shot an astonished glance at that man, her smile quickly fading.

Over in a corner, some women and girls were laughing at something. I guessed from their clothes they must be from Yihe Village, the richest in the commune with the highest production. Their villagers were better clothed than the others. I was proved right, when we went over and inquired. When I told Ashu how I had recognized them, she nodded and asked quietly, "What about us? Are we a rich village?"

"Not yet," I answered. She nodded again without comment.

Some of the women were from the second production team, known for their high cotton yield. Others were from the fifth one, known for their producing extra large potatoes. Each was claiming that the other made the greatest contribution, while not hiding the fact that they were very proud of their own work.

A tall man with greying hair came over and commented, "Don't be so humble. You've all made big contributions." This was Xu, the vice-secretary of the county Party committee. "Now you're Hu Fenlan of the second team, aren't you? Yes, I know you. And you're from the fifth team." Then turning to Ashu, he asked kindly, "And what about you? To which team do you belong?"

Startled, Ashu moved away and shook her head. "No. I don't belong." She flushed, embarrassed.

"You don't belong to what? To the commune? To these teams?" Xu laughed.

"I'm not from Yihe."

"That doesn't matter," he laughed again. Everybody joined in except Ashu who remained very serious. I couldn't fathom what was going on in the normally happy girl's mind.

Many secretaries of the various Party branches spoke at the meeting about their work and difficulties. Then up rose our old one. He began, "I'm responsible for our poor spring wheat harvest. It didn't even last us three months, and so now, we, who grow grain, are having to eat grain transported here by train from great distances. . . ." Ashu fidgeted uneasily, winding her plaits tighter and tighter round her fingers.

"Lots of people have praised our rice crop, but our yearly yield still lags behind other villages. That means we're being fed and clothed by others. We. . . ." The pipe in his hand began to quiver. I stole a glance at Ashu. She was sitting very straight, chewing at the ribbons which had been so carefully tied round her plaits and pulling out the silk.

"What are you doing, Ashu?" I nudged her. She turned and looked at me without seeing me or hearing what I was saying. She just continued to bite her ribbons, the threads floating to the floor.

What was she so engrossed in? Hardly the history of

imperialist aggression in China or some interesting story. The meeting over, she left with me. We walked through the streets and came to a highway where bicycle after bicycle passed us. "I heard your mother has asked someone to buy you a bike," I began in an effort to make conversation.

Ignoring my words, she blurted out, "Uncle is a dragon. Now I think I know what Grandpa Tiangen meant."

"I think I know. . . ." The wind blew the clouds across the evening sky. The sun set in the west as the moon rose. Another day had ended. How many new lives had begun this day throughout our vast country? Production and agriculture were forging ahead to build socialism, and young Ashu thought she understood. How significant!

The autumn harvest began after the meeting, and everyone was very busy. One night, several days later, I heard Ashu's mother grumbling about something. That reminded me. I hadn't seen Ashu for some days. What was she doing in the evenings instead of listening to my stories? I decided to go and see her soon.

I was rudely awakened the next morning by someone stumbling down the stairs next door.

"Bye, mum." It was her. Since she didn't normally get up early in the school holidays, I'd practically forgotten that noise. It felt queer to be awakened so abruptly. Next she'd start singing. I waited. Nothing. I looked out of the window. It wasn't quite dawn. Where was she going?

At daybreak I went to ask her mother. Clasping her hands, she replied, "I don't know what's got into her these days. She's made up her mind she wants to gather fertilizer and has persuaded a few friends to join her. They cut grass for two days, but then it struck her that the mud in the river bed was a much richer fertilizer. She asked me to lend them a boat. Well, I don't mind her playing about with some things, but she can't fool around with a boat needed in production. When I refused she went into a fit of sulks. This morning she went off to try and persuade my brother to lend her a boat from his village."

Of course, she'd be unsuccessful, as all the villages were using their boats. But I was glad she'd made the attempt. She was beginning to learn. Her mother ended as usual, "But really she's just a happy-go-lucky girl with no worries. . . ." For once I didn't agree with her.

With the old Party secretary, I visited the other teams to see how their work was progressing. Ashu was often in my mind, no matter how busy I was, as I wondered what she and her friends would do without a boat.

One evening, she suddenly appeared at her usual time to hear a story. I pulled her over to sit beside me. There were so many questions I wanted to ask her and I also wanted to encourage and praise her. Not knowing where to begin, I said what I hadn't intended to at all. "You've been very busy?" I asked.

She stopped smiling and was silent.

"Come, let me tell you a story." Instead of helping matters, I'd made them worse. She lowered her eyes.

I realized it was impossible to talk as we had done before. But what could we discuss? Now I fell silent.

"Do you look down on me too?" she asked, staring at me with her clear eyes. There was a new look in them which forced me to treat her with comradely respect.

"You need a boat, don't you?" I said. I wanted to help her if I could.

She shook her head. "No. Everybody's using boats. They can easily scoop up more mud than us. No, we don't need a boat to collect fertilizer."

She was very practical. I said nothing.

"We've formed a shock team," she continued defensively. She spoke rather arrogantly as if daring anyone to laugh at her. I thought of the idealism and courage of this young girl embarking on a good cause with a clear aim. The old Party secretary had said, "You're competing, whether you like it or not." Here I was, witnessing this young girl taking part in a significant competition. Although happy and moved, I didn't laugh or smile. Seeing my serious expression, Ashu relaxed and pleaded with me, "Mum listens to you. Please talk to her. She won't recognize our team or give us any work to do."

"Have you talked about this to your old Party secretary?"

"Of course! He told us we were only young primary school graduates and that we could only do a few odd jobs, but no work in the fields." She paused for a moment before continuing, "Never mind. If we wait for others to feed and clothe us, we'll just be like the worms Grandpa Tiangen talked about."

How to lead a meaningful life is a most serious question. I wanted to say, "Prove yourself capable by your actions. It's no use my talking to your mother." But afraid that was too harsh, I finally asked, "What do you plan to do now?"

"We...." she began, then thought for a moment before continuing, "Wait and see!" As she turned to leave, the green ribbons around her plaits bobbed up and down.

That night I dreamt of some carefully selected wheat seeds which grew into Ashu's face, sprouting green shoots which curled into her green ribbons....

Next morning I awoke before dawn. The birds were silent and the cock hadn't crowed yet. I lay waiting for Ashu to stumble down the stairs. She was bound to be up early since she had work to do. Daybreak and still silence next door, so I had to get up. Then I heard a voice outside my window saying, "Better send a boat to help."

"Yes, a layer of mud over a layer of this is very rich."

"They've certainly done well."

I opened the door. There was the old Party secretary with Ashu's mother. Over by the river I could see Ashu and her team of five girls pulling water chestnut vines out of the water.

"What are they playing at?" I asked Ashu's mother. The old Party secretary smiled and walked away. Giving me a reproachful glance, her mother grunted, "Collecting fertilizer." Keeping a straight face, I went with her towards the girls and called to Ashu, "What are you doing?"

"Cooking birthday noodles for Mother Earth!" she joked. Trouser legs rolled up, all the girls were fishing out the vines, twisting them around two bamboo poles like a cook taking noodles out of a pot with chopsticks.

Looking at the bedraggled girls, Ashu's mother sighed, "Well, Ashu, you're...." She stopped abruptly, choking back "a happy-go-lucky girl with no worries".

There were already several big piles of vines heaped up on the bank. Water dripped from the unpicked water chestnuts. Ashu had no time for them; she was too busy collecting more vines. But some children from the kindergarten were enjoying themselves crawling among the vines picking the water chestnuts.

"Are you happy?" I asked the children, whose pockets were bulging with water chestnuts.

"Of course they are!" Ashu answered for them. "This is really a pleasure. Look there!" She pointed to a blackboard on which was written: "Strive to work hard." Their quota and what they had already achieved was written on it also.

Ashu's mother shook her head disapprovingly at the happy girls. Perhaps she felt they should work in a more solemn way. Unconsciously, she sighed again. But before she could say anything she noticed the board and exclaimed, "Look!"

A girl erased the previous figure of vines gathered and chalked up the new one of 4,000.

"Hey, Ashu! We've come to work with you." A boat scudded over poled by the old Party secretary and with a young man holding a mud scoop.

"Let's have a contest. As you pull out the vines, we'll cover them with mud and see who wins," shouted the old man in high spirits.

"Hurrah!" the excited girls cried. "We accept your challenge." I'd never seen happy-go-lucky Ashu so joyful before.

April 1961

Translated by Wen Xue

Comradeship

OUR army troupe was to split into two and go off with the regular army. That meant our mess team would split up too for a while. Those going south would have the tougher time, as our troops were to thrust right through the enemy. The cooks accompanying them had to be the strongest. As our quartermaster was no longer young they sent him with the other force while I, only just promoted to a sergeant's rank, became acting quartermaster for the southern expedition. Of our four cooks I was given Zhu and Zhang.

It is no joke running the mess during a campaign. When the soldiers have eaten, washed their bowls and fastened them to their belts, they can set off as soon as the signal comes to advance. But we in the cook-house cannot start till we have washed the pans and packed up supplies. Then we have to outmarch the troops to get to the next halt ahead of them. Other comrades have nothing to do when they arrive but wash their feet, smoke and rest, while we weigh out fuel and straw, provision ourselves and cook. In brief, it is a gruelling revolutionary task. And this time we would be outwitting the enemy and changing our positions all the time.

Having Zhu and Zhang put fresh heart into me, however. Both were splendid workers, though no longer young. And while utterly unlike, they got along together as well as turnips and beancurd.

Zhang, at forty-one, was slightly the older of the two, a real mountain of a man, incredibly good-natured. Like many good-natured fellows, he was slow on the uptake and it took him three sentences to express a simple idea. Give him a steamed bun and he would just grin at you. Give him a punch and the answer was still a grin. (Not when he was dealing with the enemy, mind you.) Zhu, on the other hand, was lean and quick, a hard, conscientious worker. He had served in the regular army, fought very bravely, and been wounded several times. But he was easily roused and then he passed cutting remarks in a loud, angry voice. No respecter of persons, he let you know exactly, down to the last detail, what you had done to displease him. This was not Zhang's way and he listened, grinning, while Zhu had his say. So when the two were together, Zhang had a lively time while Zhu found things quiet. But they never fell out. Having the two was like having a civil official and military commander who could between them cope with anything. This made my job so much the simpler.

Just before we set out, however, the army command decided we were short-handed and sent us a reinforcement. So far so good. But when I saw our new helper, my heart sank.

It was Young Zhou, a messenger from regimental headquarters, known as the Handy Man. He came swinging along, singing,

> Under the moon, she waits for you to come. . . .
> Guess who? Your mum!

He bounded cheerfully in to report his arrival. His army tunic hung loosely over his thighs. He had thick eyebrows, black, sparkling, intelligent eyes, and he stood to attention looking very alert. Young as he was, he tackled every job with great determination. He was a grand "little devil",* a fine comrade. But this combination of the three of them complicated matters and was going to make things difficult for me.

To explain why, I had better start with Young Zhou. He was just sixteen, the youngest in the whole troupe. A messenger for the troupe, he actually had a hand in all that went on. If the stage work was busy, he would brush the back-cloth and nail it up or go out to borrow costumes. If we were short of actors for a crowd scene, he liked nothing better than to rouge his cheeks and perform on the stage. Hence his nickname the Handy Man. He was a general favourite with the whole crowd, but Zhang in our cook-house was his special friend. Zhang liked to smoke and if, as sometimes happened, we camped in a place where we were cut off from supplies, Young Zhou would show extraordinary ingenuity in getting the local children to rout out tobacco; or he would eye the cigarette tins of the officers to whom he delivered messages, and if they gave him a couple of cigarettes he would race back to slip the crumpled booty into Zhang's hand. Zhang for his part did all he could for the boy from teaching him how to fasten his puttees to giving him political education. Each month after our pay was issued, he did not feel happy till he had spent something on Young Zhou. And the boy, who looked on him as a father, sometimes

---

* The name given to youngsters in the people's army.

played up to him. Nothing wrong in that, it is common enough in the revolutionary ranks; but the complication arose because it was not just the two of them involved. And if it had just been a question of Zhu and Young Zhou, that would have been simple too. No, the problem was the three of them together.

The trouble had started before New Year when our troops were resting and regrouping at Yang Village. One day Zhang and I went into town to buy a great pile of celery, turnips, bamboo shoots, vermicelli, beef and so on. As soon as we were back, Zhang quietly told Young Zhou to come to the cook-house that evening.

At dusk, lustily singing *Under the Moon*, Young Zhou arrived cheerfully anticipating a treat of some sort. And sure enough, Zhang, smiling all over his face, produced a bowl of piping hot vermicelli soup garnished with pork and shallots and smelling delicious. Young Zhou was very partial to vermicelli and, knowing that Zhang had made this specially for him, he sat down and fell to without further ado, swallowing the soup with gusto. Zhang, his pipe between his lips, sat on a mat beside him, a satisfied spectator.

They were blissfully happy, one eating, the other watching, when who should burst in but Zhu. He had no special liking for Young Zhou and nothing against him either. But it annoyed him to see the boy eating there, in the evening of all times, and he pulled a long face, suspecting Zhang of using army rations to treat his friend, and these were difficult times when each man's ration was strictly limited. So he asked:

"Old Zhang, did you buy vermicelli today for the troops?"

Had it been me, my mind would have jumped to the vermicelli in Young Zhou's bowl and I should have given a prompt explanation. But not so Zhang. Slowly removing the pipe from his mouth, he pointed to a corner. "Yes! Look there." Zhu turned and saw a great heap of vermicelli, apparently untouched. He fixed his eyes on Young Zhou's bowl and blustered:

"It's not right, Old Zhang, to treat friends with army supplies!"

That was blunt enough and anyone else would have taken offence. But Zhang unhurriedly tapped the bowl of his pipe as he agreed, "No, of course not!"

Meanwhile Young Zhou, holding his chopsticks, had stopped eating, his whole face scarlet. He was a cheerful lad, but once his temper was roused he did not mince matters. The atmosphere was electric.

If Zhu had only had the least sense of perspective, he should have known from Zhang's honourable record that nothing could be amiss. But Zhu was not the fellow to think things out. Exasperated by his friend's vague answer, he demanded outright, "Where did that vermicelli Young Zhou's eating come from?"

"That. . . ." Far from flaring up, Zhang only grinned at Zhu as he fumbled in his pocket for a slip of paper, spread it out flat and passed it over. "See, there's the receipt. I bought an extra two ounces. . . ." Before he could finish, Young Zhou put in:

"Old Zhu, why do you use the eyes of the old society to look at people? That's not comradely!" His voice was trembling, he was quivering with fury. Mention of "the old society" set Zhu off too. "Comrade!" he bellowed. "If everybody was like you, our cook-house would turn into a restaurant and the army oil, salt and fuel would soon be finished!"

"I won't eat it then!" cried Young Zhou. And slapping down his chopsticks he jumped up and marched angrily out.

Zhang, who had had no chance to get a word in, wrinkled his forehead and said ruefully, "See here, though! See here! This won't do." This was his usual reaction to any misunderstanding, as if his "See here!" would make the other party see light all of a sudden.

So now Zhu directed his anger against Zhang. "What am I supposed to see? A fine soldier you've trained!"

"See here, though, you ought to make sure of your facts before you talk. Look, here's two ounces of oil I bought. How could I just take public property?" Zhang produced a bowl of oil. He was most upset. The vermicelli he had been so glad to buy had caused such unpleasantness. Worst of all, it had made bad blood between two comrades. And he was at the bottom of this, the one most to blame. So with a sigh he admitted, "Yes, it's my fault!"

Although Zhu was still smouldering, this took the wind out of his sails and he flung himself down to sleep.

There the matter should have dropped. But the next evening a concert party was coming from another unit to give a performance and at noon, as ill luck would have it, Young Zhou was told to take a message to army headquarters. That was over thirty *li* away. He would not be back in time to see the show. He looked so downcast that Zhang took pity on him and persuaded the quartermaster to lend Young Zhou our big black mare. The lad rushed joyfully to the backyard to untether her.

"Stop that!" said Zhu, who was there, not lifting his head. "She's got saddle-sores."

"I've the quartermaster's permission!" Young Zhou went ahead.

"I don't care if you have!" Zhu straightened up. It was true the mare was not fit to be ridden, but Zhu's tongue, always blunt, was more caustic than ever today on account of his low opinion of Young Zhou. "You're in army uniform: try to act like a soldier. Can't you even walk a few *li*?"

Young Zhou flushed red with rage, he whirled round and stamped off. After that, he was convinced Zhu was biassed against him, and this tangle had never been straightened out since.

So that was how things stood between the three. Keep them apart and all was well. Put them together and it was a bad look-out for me. But Young Zhou had been assigned to us, and how could I send him back? With a sinking heart, I told them to pack up and get ready to leave.

As soon as we had issued dry rations and the order came to fall in, the trouble started.

Young Zhou, after fastening his own pack, put beside it a hundred-catty scales belonging to the mess and a sack of grain which he meant to carry on the march. But the moment he left the cook-house, Zhang shouldered these things himself. Zhu had quite a weight to carry, and he frowned when he saw Zhang's heavy load and nothing in Young Zhou's place but a small pack. When the lad came back, Zhu said to Zhang, "Give some of your stuff to Young Zhou. He's been sent here to work."

At first Young Zhou did not understand. When he caught on he lost his temper, but he started sulking instead of troubling to explain.

It had not come to a quarrel, but still I was worried. If this went on it would interfere with our work, and conditions were going to get steadily worse, which made solidarity doubly important. They could not be allowed to go on like this. They must make it up. I decided that as soon as we made camp I would have a talk with each of them separately.

We marched all night, not making camp till it was light. Then we had to prepare a meal and snatch time to rest. And the further we went behind the enemy lines, the more trouble we had from the landlords' militia, who kept sniping at us. It was harder, too, to get the fuel and grain we needed. What with one thing and another, I never got round to tackling their problem. True, there was no open squabble, but they barely spoke to each other. The cook-house was as cheerful as a tomb.

We marched for four or five days. Then getting on for midnight one day, the order came back for absolute quiet and "No breaking ranks!" We were approaching a highway with enemy for several *li* on both sides of it. The men must keep close together, no one must lag a step behind.

Just before coming to this highway, however, we had crossed a stream and then it was that I noticed Zhu had disappeared. The troops were marching full speed ahead and our regimental command refused to leave anyone behind for liaison. I started cursing our black mare because she was the reason for Zhu's falling behind.

Zhu doted on that big black mare. He led her on every march and the first thing he did on arrival was to feed her. Because his precious charge had saddle-sores the previous day, he had taken off her load to carry it himself. Knowing we were to cross the highway that night at full speed, we all urged Zhu against this, all except Young Zhou who as usual made no comment. But long arguments failed to dissuade Zhu from taking the mare's load and giving her his small pack in exchange.

His falling behind at such a time had us all worried. We comforted ourselves with the thought that he knew the way and where we were to camp. At the worst, he would arrive a little late.

We reached our destination before dawn. But barely had we gone to our billets when there came emergency orders: we were to march on by day! I was appalled and Zhang, who was fetching water, plunged his bucket down to stand rooted to the ground. "But what about Old Zhu?" he asked at last.

Young Zhou, taking off his pack, sat down without a word, his eyes fixed on the flickering lamplight. After thinking it over, I told them to pack up while I went to headquarters for instructions. Regimental headquarters were ready to go into action and said they could not send anyone to wait for Zhu. Also it was out of the question to leave word of our destination. That being so, it was up to Zhu whether he could rejoin us or not. Very depressed, I returned to tell the two others.

Zhang stared blankly, while Young Zhou leapt to his feet and went out. The horizon was growing light, in the distance one or two stray shots rang out, some signals for falling in were already sounding. Young Zhou stared down the path to the village, and stood there motionless. Not till the order came to fall in did he walk slowly back, pick up his kit and grain sack, and stride into the yard. He took Zhu's pack off the mare and shouldered it himself, then led the big mare to the assembly ground. Zhang watched him in distress and tried to take Zhu's pack. But Young Zhou shook his head and trudged off, his eyes on the ground.

When we stopped in a village at noon to rest, headquarters called an emergency meeting of regimental cadres to explain that we were going into battle at once and the rest time should be used to lighten loads — no pack must weigh more than four catties. When I went back to announce this, Zhang got the scales and weighed each man's kit in turn. His own pack was the heaviest, the second heaviest that left by Zhu. Zhang opened his up and removed some old clothes and things he would not be needing immediately. I opened Zhu's pack in his absence, since orders were orders, and left him a change of clothes and a sheet, but piled everything else on the ground.

Standing there looking at the various objects, Zhang said, "Old Zhu bought this himself and has hardly ever worn it. Let me keep it for him! . . . He brought that from home. I'll take it for him." Then he picked up a faded, dirty uniform. "Let's hang on to this too. He'll need it when next we halt." That reminded us of one of Zhu's peculiarities. Each time we went into battle he insisted on looking smart and often put on a new uniform, no matter whether he was to be a stretcher-bearer or march through rain and mud. But when we stopped and had a chance to spruce up, he liked to wear tattered old clothes. If his own were worn out, he would try to exchange his new uniform for someone else's old one. That way he felt more comfortable and could work better. This old outfit he had not had time to wash was one he had traded for a new uniform. Young Zhou, who had been watching too, now came over and picked up all Zhu's belongings, which he put back in Zhu's pack. "Here, lighten mine!" he said, and opened his own. There was really nothing redundant in his pack. But he took out his sheet, shirt and even his precious song-book and dropped them on the ground. For two years he had carried that dog-eared song-book about, and from it he had learned *Under the Moon*. Presently he pulled out a summer uniform Zhang had altered to fit him, but he thought too good to wear. It was still quite new. Weighing it in his hands, with a surreptitious look at Zhang he put it on the ground.

There was no more he could discard, while several of Zhu's belongings were not essentials. I persuaded him to throw out two tattered jackets, but he firmly refused to jettison Zhu's wine flask. In the end, behind Young Zhou's back, Zhang picked up his song-book and new uniform and put them in his own pack, then reduced its weight by weeding out more of his own things.

We set off in the afternoon and marched till after midnight. Under these conditions, there was no sleep for the mess team. We set straight about getting provisions and making breakfast. After that I was so tired that I found a door-board and stretched out on it. Zhang and Young Zhou sat there stiffly, however, declaring that they had no time to sleep. They had nothing to do, of course, but were worrying about Zhu.

Because they would not sleep, neither could I. We sat facing each other and our hearts were heavy.

Young Zhou in the doorway was frowning thoughtfully. Zhang pulled on his pipe till it sputtered. Both were sunk in gloom. I dozed off and must have slept for nearly an hour when Zhang shook me awake and panted, "See here, though! See here! . . ."

"What's up?" I asked, alarmed by his expression. Slowly pointing to the stool where Young Zhou had been sitting, he told me the lad had gone and was nowhere to be found. But a peasant had seen a young soldier leaving the village.

"It's my fault," said Zhang, tears in his eyes. "For two days I've known he's been hankering to do this. But what if we set off again now?"

Yes, I had foreseen trouble too from Young Zhou's manner. Not stopping to speak, I untethered the mare in the yard, jumped on her back, and gave her a slap that sent her cantering down the road we had travelled the previous evening. I fumed as I rode. Little devil! No sense of discipline at all! He let himself be carried away by his feelings with no thought for anything else! What if the army moved on? What if he met the landlords' militia? He would die for nothing! Sweating, I spurred on the mare, riding helter-skelter for half an hour or more. Still there was no sign of the boy and I began to wonder whether, instead of looking for Zhu, he had just found himself somewhere to sleep. I reined in and mopped my face, meaning to turn back. Our troops might already be on the move by now! Just then, looking up, I caught sight of a black speck on a hill in front. I headed the mare that way. Yes, it was Young Zhou. He was sitting on a rock facing away from me, shaking with sobs. Instead of hauling him over the coals as I had intended, I simply called his name. He just buried his head on my shoulder and really broke down.

"Old Zhu will never make it now!" he sobbed.

I was pretty shaken by his tears myself. Patting him on the shoulder, I said, "Must have some casualties in a revolution." As if to confirm this, two shots sounded in the distance. At once Young Zhou took a grip on himself and stood stock-still gazing down the hill as if expecting Zhu to appear the next minute, an enemy at his heels. But apart from the grass rustling in the wind there was no sign of life — no Zhu, no enemy. Young Zhou said hoarsely, "He'd take a couple of the bastards with him, Old Zhu would!" And he started slowly back with me.

"Didn't you say you'd never hit it off with Old Zhu? Why are you sticking up for him all of a sudden?"

"We may not hit it off, but we're comrades, aren't we?" He shot me a steady glance.

"If he comes back, will you treat him decently?"

Young Zhou did not answer at once. But after we had gone some distance, he suddenly said, "Just a minute." He broke away to the side of the road, found a piece of smooth soil at the foot of a rock, and wrote on the ground with a twig:

Under the moon, she waits for you to come. . . .
Guess who? Your mum!

Then he added a verse not in the original. "Turn west, then south, to find her!" This done, he turned to me saying, "He may come through all right, after all!"

"Of course. Hurry now! Want the rest to leave without us?" So it ended up with me comforting him as I escorted him back. And luckily we found our troops still there.

We did not move on till late that night and marched over ten *li* before making camp. The troops in front were already in action, and it looked as if we would be here for two or three days. So first thing in the morning we went out to forage for hay and grain, buy vegetables and oil. I was hard at work when Zhang rushed in with a broad grin on his face, oil dripping from the jar in his hand, as pointing outside he cried, "See here now! Just see! . . ." Rather than wait for his slow explanation, I ran to the door and saw Zhu had come back!

He was carrying a battered wicker crate and had mended his broken carrying-pole with a branch. In one hand he clutched a chopper picked up goodness knows where. He was covered with mud, his hair seemed to have grown much longer in the last few days, his face was darker and thinner, and there was dried mud on his forehead. Only the fire in his eyes was unchanged. He stood there grinning sheepishly while Zhang smiled at him through tears. Zhu's eyes reddened too, but he bellowed, "What are you crying for? Is this worth crying about?"

Before I could go out to welcome him, Young Zhou dashed out to fling his arms round Zhu, who blinked back his tears and muttered gruffly, "Let a chap put down his load, won't you!" As Zhang took it from him, Zhu turned to Young Zhou to say, "I saw the message you left me!"

Carrying the crate and grinning foolishly, Zhang chortled, "See now! See now! . . ."

At last I could set my mind at rest. Zhu was back, no mediation would be needed, the army was not on the march, and we had our supplies. That evening after a good bath I decided to turn in early. When I reached the cook-house door I heard Zhu say pugnaciously, "It's no good, I tell you, coddling him the way you do!" That gave me a nasty jolt. What was wrong now? I peeped through a crack in the door and saw Young Zhou sound asleep. Zhu and Zhang, astride a long bench, were making the sandals of cloth and straw which were the most popular footwear at that time.

"All right, then. Just start them for him and make him finish them," continued Zhu.

"Why are you finishing yours in that case?" Zhang stopped and chuckled, pulling on his pipe.

"I'm finishing this one so that he has something to copy." Aware, no doubt, how feeble this sounded, Zhu threw a stern glance at Zhang. "Coddling won't produce good soldiers."

I slipped in while they were talking and found Zhu had nearly finished his sandal while Zhang's was lying there half done. Not wanting to disturb them, I lay down. Soon there was nothing to break the silence but the sputtering of Zhang's pipe and the sound Zhu made tearing strips of cloth while he crooned *Under the Moon.*

May 1961

Translated by Gladys Yang

Between Two Seas

MY destination was the East Sea coast, due south of Male Bay, and here I was.

Before I came here I was told that you could walk that eastern coast in the rain without leaving footprints and after the rain a layer of frosty salt soon appeared on the surface. It was barren alkaline land, an expanse of white all the year round, white for scores of years. But whether white or black it was still land, a vast tract stretching as far as eye could see. How many farmers it fired with daring dreams!

And twenty years ago a farmer named Liben, driven by famine from his native home, brought his old parents and six children here. The landlord told him, "Till this land, and I won't charge you rent for the first three years." Liben looked at this vast white expanse, his heart beating fast, his face flushed in anticipation. Three years without having to pay rent! If he could improve the soil a little the first year, in the second year and the third he could do better. Beautiful visions of his six children's future flashed before his dazzled eyes. He was well aware that others before him had failed here. Still he stooped to taste a pinch of the soil, which was salty and bitter. However, he was strong and determined enough to take a gamble on this vast pitiless stretch of white coast. He pulled down his old house and rebuilt it by the seaside. Nearly everyone in his family worked on the land. He sold whatever they had of value to get a little money to buy fertilizer. In a word, he staked the lives and property of their family of ten on this land. He brushed aside all warnings and advice, trusting to his own hard work, convinced that any land warmed by the sun and washed by the rain and dew must produce good crops if only enough hard work was put into it.

The tides ebbed and flowed. In quick succession three years came to an end. The eastern coast was still a stretch of white. The only difference was that a small plot of land bore cotton stems no thicker than chopsticks. Liben was reduced to skin and bones. For three years the whole family had had to subsist on the crabs and rhubarb roots which Haida, his fifth son, caught and dug up on the sea-shore.

When the three years were up, Liben and his family pulled down their house and moved away. Before leaving, Liben gazed at the coast with tears in his eyes and said, "My strength and money are gone, I can do no more. But I'm sure this land could grow crops."

Now a pioneer team made up of young members of the commune was farming this stretch of coast. Apart from growing cotton, wheat, melons and paddy on the white alkaline soil, they had raised fish and planted fruit trees. Last of all I was told that the team leader was Haida, Liben's son, who had once again rebuilt his house, the only property his father left him, by the sea-side. The young folk had set up a new village there.

A flock of white seagulls suddenly took flight nearby and whirred with slanting wings over my head. In front of me glittered a white belt — the sea. I half ran to the shore and there I saw two seas. One with dazzling waves and white sails in the distance, the gulls overhead looking like stars that somebody had scattered in the sky. These faithful companions of all navigators were drifting with wings unfurled from this sea to another: a rippling green sea of wheat. It was early spring. The wheat had not ripened yet. Nevertheless, the field was a sea of green stretching to the azure sky. Clouds were scudding before the wind. The East Sea seemed to be booming: "This land could grow crops." No, it was not the voice of the sea but that of Liben and Haida, the voice perhaps of two generations of peasants.

I wanted to meet Haida and the rest of his team to see if they were as husky as I imagined. But where did they live? Was that an island beyond the green sea? No, it was a shelter belt, behind which a mass of peach blossom or apricot blossom showed pink.

In front of the blossoming trees I found the team's headquarters. But nobody was in. It happened to be their day off. The few stockmen who had stayed to feed the animals told me that Haida and the others would be back that evening and led me inside a very small office. I sat down behind a desk by the window, my head touching the loudspeaker hanging on the wall. It occurred to me that this small house might be the very one that had been pulled down three times and rebuilt by the seaside. Through the window one saw the boundless sea. Looking at the green sea in the dusk, my mind turned to Liben and Haida. I wondered what magic Haida had that he was able to make the goal for which his parents had vainly risked all they had,

including their lives. The green sea became a dark blur
and a solemn march struck up, softly but clearly.   I
found it was coming from the loudspeaker behind me;
the commune was broadcasting the day's last programme
of music. Just then, bicycle bells rang outside the gate.
The members of the pioneer team were back, Haida
among them. A short young fellow with full lips and a
lock of hair falling forward over one eyebrow, Haida
did not quite fit my conception of him. And I bombard-
ed him with so many questions that at first he was at a
loss as to where to begin. After a while he said in all
seriousness, "In the autumn of 1958 the Youth League
of our commune called on us to organize a pioneer
team. More than forty young men volunteered. Later
they elected me to be the team leader. . . ."   When
he started, his comrades listened to him out of curiosity,
but soon enough they went to another table and started
a game of cards, since Haida's account held nothing
new for them.

"When we arrived here, we planted wheat. The next
year we reaped an average yield of. . . ."   He took
out his notebook to check up the figure. He was giving
me an accurate, detailed survey when the "battle" at
the other table reached a climax. The onlookers were
shouting advice, some were even grabbing at cards. The
packed office was seething. Those originally seated had
leapt to their feet and their places had been promptly
seized by others.   It was difficult to distinguish the
players from the onlookers. A gay party was under
way.

It was hard to concentrate on what Haida was saying,
but I could hardly drop the subject I had just raised.

I asked, "What was your biggest difficulty when you started reclaiming the wasteland?"

"The biggest difficulty?" Haida had no answer ready. Smiling at me and scratching his head he began to think hard. He looked as if this were the biggest difficulty he had yet faced.

"Believe me, two extra batteries will make the sound louder," said one young fellow to another. The two of them were fiddling with the loudspeaker.

"I know how to do it. Just tighten that thing there and it will improve the volume," said a youngster with tousled hair. And no sooner said than done. After a sudden shriek the loudspeaker was silent. Though nobody had seemed to pay any attention to the music before, now that the loudspeaker had ceased to make any sound everybody noticed it. All turned to look at the youngster with tousled hair who flushed in embarrassment. Silence reigned in the room.

"Oh, I know the difficulty." Haida had found one at last. "When we first came here there was no fresh water. Our porridge tasted bitter."

"How did you get round that?" I asked.

"Get round it? By digging a canal." Haida seemed surprised that I should not know how to solve this problem of water. And he added, "By bringing in fresh water from Male Bay. We killed two birds with one stone — got ourselves drinking water and a good means of transport." He spoke of digging a canal as if it were the easiest thing in the world, like building with toy bricks. So that difficulty was no difficulty at all. I asked, "Had you no other difficulties?"

"Of course we had," said a tough-looking young man who had just been defeated in the card game, before

Haida was ready to reply. "Soon after we arrived here there was typhoon and downpour. The straw on our thatched huts was blown off like willow-down. We stayed indoors holding up umbrellas."

"The cooking was the best part to watch," put in another.

"Ha, at that time we had this wretch as our cook." The tough card-player patted the head of the lad who had been trying to repair the loudspeaker. "He behaved like the king of all cooks. When it rained he made three men hold umbrellas for him. One for the cooking pan, another for the firewood, and the third for His Majesty's head. Imagine what a lively time we had."

I was so impressed by their youthful, revolutionary optimism that I wanted to spring to my feet and pay some tribute to these fine youngsters. But they had talked only about their living conditions. How about the land? How had they made it yield?

"How could it help but yield?" said the tough young fellow quickly before any of the others could get a word in. "Tractors came round the beach and roared up and down the whole farm. When we wanted fertilizer, boatfuls came. Sheep and cattle were grazed here to give us more manure. Now we have all the fertilizer we need, chemical or natural. A small heifer we brought with us then will soon be a grandmother."

Suddenly the loudspeaker came to life again. The volume had certainly increased. Everybody cheered. The young repairer smiled, wiping the sweat from his forehead, happiness written on his face. Haida nodded at me, grinning, as if to say, "You see what we are like here. Nothing else to speak about."

Outside the wind was sweeping over the green sea. The wheat was shooting up, the fruit trees were blossoming. A voice seemed to be saying, "This land could grow crops."

May 1961

Translated by Zhang Su

A Badly Edited Story

THE first thing I must make clear is that this is a badly edited story. However, I'll do my best to make it smoother and more logical so as to avoid confusing readers.

1. He may have been slapping his thighs and humming a tune, but he was still worried

It all happened in 1958 when the neighbouring communes and production brigades one after another declared that the yield of one *mu* of their paddy fields was as much as twelve or thirteen thousand catties. Red flags fluttered everywhere, gongs sounded, drums rolled. Good news kept pouring in from all directions, and flocks of visitors came and went.

Gan, the commune committee Party secretary, was anxious to catch up with the others and talked for three full nights to persuade Old Han, branch Party secretary of the first brigade, to launch a "satellite". Finally the first brigade went into action. It was about time, thought Gan. In for a penny, in for a pound — he would beat them all. He had a dozen *mu*'s rice moved to one *mu* and then announced that their yield had reached sixteen thousand catties! The whole commune was thrown into a commotion. A pine-and-cypress archway was erected, drums and gongs were beaten and the

high-yield patch was ringed with red flags. A report
was being prepared. Since visitors swarmed in, a couple
of dozen peasants were called on to act as guides. It
was really exciting! Nothing could put them more in
the limelight. The commune's name became known
throughout the county, and was soon in a news bulletin
sent to the provincial government and to the Central
Party Committee. But it wasn't very clear who had
been cited in it. Anyway, not long after, Gan was promoted to deputy Party secretary of the county committee and people assumed it had probably been his name
in the bulletin. But that's just a guess, there's no proper
evidence.

In the beginning both the cadres and peasants of
the first brigade found it all rather interesting and
amusing, but before long, when large grain purchases
were requisitioned by the state they began to worry.
They had to deliver public grain in proportion to what
they'd claimed they'd achieved. That was a lot less en-
joyable! Now the peasants were all like ants in a fry-
ing pan. To try and save the situation a man called
Longevity, deputy leader of the third team as well as
head orchard keeper, appeared.

His real name was Tian Shouben, but the villagers
just called him Longevity because of his appearance:
he had kind eyes beneath bushy brows, a big bald head,
and always wore a pleasant expression. He never got
into a bad temper and nothing ever seemed to annoy
him. He looked like the Longevity God you often see
in glass cases in country households. Actually, he wasn't
as old as he seemed. He was only sixty-six, and a
veteran Party member. During the war, he had worked
as a liaison man for the Party. He wasn't much of a

talker and whenever he opened his mouth, people started to laugh. He could never work out why. He was an
earnest and serious sort, and never cracked jokes. He
didn't know how to deal with them. He guessed that
was just the way young people behaved these days.
They probably just wanted to laugh anyway and simply used him as an excuse. This gradually became a
habit. Others thought he was a bit of an old fogey. His
nickname hinted as much. Still, everybody liked his
company and except at Party meetings, not many
thought of him as a Party member. But he himself was
very much aware of his Party membership and discipline.

As soon as he came out of the orchard, he saw four
carts parked on the village road loaded with sacks of
grain and decorated with colourful banners. The first
horse had a large red rosette on its head and a streamer
was stretched along the cart bearing the words "Hand-
ing in a high grain yield is a great honour". There was
also a set of drums, gongs, and cymbals on the cart.
Everything was ready, there was only the carter missing. If you asked anybody to drive it, they'd take to
their heels at once. The sun was already well up and
soon crowds of visitors would arrive, but they still
couldn't get anyone to move. Party Secretary Han
stamped his feet in frustration, and seeing Longevity
was as delighted as if he'd spotted some rare treasure.
He hurriedly put the whip in Longevity's hand and
urged, "Hurry up, drive the carts to the grain station.
We're late and Gan's already mad at us."

While he was talking, visitors started to arrive. Old
Han turned round and hurried over to greet them with
a broad smile. If only Longevity would crack his whip

and the four carts would roll out of the village against the tide of visitors, how wonderful that would be! But instead Longevity tugged at the hem of Han's coat, the long whip cradled in his hand. He discreetly made a number eight with his thumb and forefinger for Han to see.

"You want eight people? I'll give you ten. Pick them yourself, I'll keep their work points for them." Having said this, Han shook hands with his visitors. Usually he would first take them to the high-yield plot to have a look and then afterwards show them to the old ancestral hall to rest for a bit. They would be given towels dipped in cold well water and offered green tea while they listened to an account of the commune's feats.

Among the visitors that day, there was one who asked a lot of detailed questions and who was probably an agronomist. He plucked a rice ear, counted the grains and wrapped them up, saying he would weigh them later. Then he examined a tuft, counted the number of stalks and asked what the distance was between rows and tufts. Plied with so many questions, the brigade leader sweated profusely till his white coat was almost soaked. But the visitor pressed further and asked with evident surprise and curiosity, "It's so densely planted, how did you solve the problem of aeration?"

"We, uh, with bamboo poles. . . ." As Han murmured, someone at the back came to his rescue, "And electric fans! Don't you town people use electric fans these days? Just blow the air in!"

It was Longevity! Instead of setting off, he'd followed the Party secretary, whip in hand. But his explanation almost made the guide burst out laughing. An anxious Han whirled round, raised his eyebrows and nodded his head urging him to go. Longevity of course knew what he meant, but he promptly made an eight again in front of his chest. No one knew if Han saw the gesture or not, since he turned to face another visitor who was anxiously asking if the village had electricity.

"No, well . . . we've got a small motor, from our tractor. . . ." Old Han attempted to cover it up, and then muttered angrily to a peasant standing next to him, "Tell Longevity to get a move on!"

After looking at the high-yield plot, the visitors were shepherded into the ancestral hall to listen to the report. Now all Han had to do was to read out a written speech, and he felt much more at ease. As he described the villagers' delight at the high yield, he even spontaneously composed a little rhyme:

> Four years' grain in one year's work.
> What a wonderful life we're bound to have.
> I slap my thigh and hum a song,
> Communism's coming won't be long.

Glimpsing somebody lurking outside the window, he looked up. It was Longevity again, watching him with that whip still in his hand. Seeing Old Han looking in his direction, he eagerly held up his fingers in an eight. Old Han had no alternative but to excuse himself and go outside. Grabbing Longevity by the arm he led him over to a tall elm tree in the middle of the compound and when they were safely out of sight demanded, "What are you up to? Why on earth do you keep making that sign?"

"Well, it's because I want us to be hale and hearty,

have a good appetite and sleep well that I'm worried. Old Han, everyone says we can't send off four carts of grain. If we do our daily grain ration would only be eight ounces!" He emphasized his point by making a large eight with his fingers.

Old Han sighed, pulled up his coat lapel and wiped his perspiring forehead. "What can I do, the state grain purchase is calculated according to output. Secretary Gan says we have to hand in the grain as promised."

"Talk to him again, he knows perfectly well how we got the high yield."

"I have, but he insists." Han was getting annoyed.

"Well . . . we'll have to be patient and try again. Right?"

To illustrate his own patience, Longevity wore a big smile, arching his eyebrows. "We're responsible for several hundred people. How can they get by on eight ounces a day?"

Han frowned and kept shaking his head without saying a word. You had to compromise, something Longevity would never learn. He was still making that sign, though less emphatically, while patting Han on the chest with the back of his hand. "This much just won't do. But Secretary Gan couldn't let several hundred people starve, could he?"

"Don't go against the tide, old man, do as you're told, anything we say is useless."

Han vented his pent-up anger and frustration. Knowing he didn't really mean it, Longevity kept smiling, "Subordinates must obey their superiors, I know that. But can't we explain to them about our difficulties?"

Han had reached the end of his patience. "Then you go and try! I haven't got the time!" he roared.

He left Longevity standing there, scratching his stubbly chin. "No way out," he mused, "okay, I'll go and see him, but the grain has to be sent to the depot first. Whether they agree or not, we still have to obey orders. If he accepts my argument, then we'll just drive the grain back. Anyway, you can't boil dumplings and noodles in the same pot."

Having made up his mind, he got three old men to help and drove the carts to the commune headquarters. And when he got there they told him that Secretary Gan was now not only secretary of the commune Party committee but also deputy secretary of the county Party committee. At the moment he was away making a report to the provincial authorities.

"Nothing else we can do but to run these beasts into the ground and go to the county seat." Instead of feeling deflated, Longevity became even more energetic. He took off his coat and mounted the cart with only a coarse cloth vest on. The other three, however, wanted to go back.

"Forget it, Longevity," one said. "Who are we to go off seeing county heads? What an idea!"

"Ha, you're wrong there," retorted Longevity, knitting his long eyebrows. "We're going to go to the county government. Isn't it our government?"

"Secretary Gan's talking to big shots from the provincial government, what business have we got there?"

"You're wrong again. Provincial leaders aren't guests, they're there to work. Work for us. Maybe our problems can be solved on the spot and they'll tell us to take the grain back. We'll let Han see how effective useless old men can be." He jumped on to the cart, cracked his whip and they moved off to the county Party offices.

Longevity's assumption was neither totally right nor totally wrong. When they got to the committee's court-yard gate they were stopped. They turned over their grain and then went back to wait at the reception. After two hours Gan finally appeared. Before Longevity could even open his mouth, Gan said soberly, "First I must give you a piece of my mind. You're too short-sighted, all you care about are a few handfuls of grain. Now one day equals twenty years, we're rushing to-wards communism. If you lose a step, you'll lag behind. As a veteran revolutionary, you ought to respond even more readily to the Party's call. Think of the war, did we used to talk about trifles like seven or eight ounces of grain then?"

The tirade made Longevity speechless and he lower-ed his head. He was silent in the empty cart on the way back. He fixed the whip to the side and let the horse go as it wished. Narrowing his eyes, he began to chew over what Gan said. Every word was true of course, they'd never complained about shortages of food in those days. For a better future, they'd even fought on empty stomachs, and no one had ever protested. It looked as though that better life was still to come. But when? That Gan hadn't told them. The old Gan would never have been like that, he wouldn't have said that. Well, who knows. Maybe I'm too old to keep up with the times. I'm old and backward now. He couldn't figure it out. As the cart jostled along, he fell asleep.

2. Old Gan was not necessarily Secretary Gan or perhaps he was, but Longevity remained Longevity

At the very beginning of the winter of 1947, the poor got a full blast of freezing cold weather. Even your tongue got frozen stiff. They were in an area of seesaw battles, and land reform hadn't started then. It was already dark by the time Longevity got home after a full day of running about. Wrapped in a tattered cotton-padded coat, he had a rope round his waist and a small basket on his shoulder for collecting dung. As soon as he entered the house, he asked his wife, "Anything to eat? Give me something, I'm freezing." He put his basket down and squatted in front of the stove. Stoking the fire he roasted his shivering body.

This wife of his was a tenacious type who never gave in to hardship, but she was also a nagging woman. Longevity put it this way: "She's a kind-hearted woman who says too much but she's usually right."

She was upset to see her man trembling with cold. "Didn't you have anything to eat all day?" she asked.

"Where could I have eaten?" replied Longevity, rubbing his face vigorously with his warmed hands. She quickly removed the lid from a pot to reveal a bowl of corn and sweet potato leaf porridge sitting in warm water. To show her concern, she took down a basket and produced a large sorghum pancake. She broke off a big piece and thrust it at him, "Any news?"

"Some of the armed landlords corp returned with a whole regiment of troops and two hay cutters."

"Why don't you inform the county guerrillas immediately?"

"I'm no fool, I've just been to Old Gan, haven't I?"

Longevity raised his eyebrows and picked up the bowl, but then put it back down before even taking a sip. He took out four grain ration bags and looked down. "Old Gan and the others have decided to head behind the enemy tonight to avoid a fresh attack, then fight back later. When they get to a place they don't know, they'll have difficulty finding food. . . ."

His wife knew immediately what he meant, and before he could finish she opened the small wooden chest and took out a sack of sorghum. "This is all we've got and it's freezing cold. We can manage without it, but what about the children? It's up to you."

"We've got our problems, that's true enough," Longevity continued, his eyes still on the ground. "But I'm in the Party. Besides, if we feel cold or hungry, we can build a fire or find some wild plants. They're going to a really far-away place, they won't know where to sleep or what to eat. But they're doing it for us, aren't they?"

"Hey! Shut your trap and fill those bags. I say two sentences and you start a lecture, who says the revolution isn't for poor people."

"Exactly! You've get a good head on your shoulders, it's my fault for rabbitting on. Honestly, this isn't enough for a meal for them. But it shows our concern and will come handy when they need it. Old Gan will come by here in a minute, I told him to stop in to pick up some grain." As he went on he and his wife filled up three out of the four bags with all the sorghum they had.

"There should be enough to fill all four. One bag takes three catties, four take twelve." Holding the empty bag, he turned round, looked at the ground and said, "I remember we had fifteen catties, what happened?"

"What do you think we've been eating the last few days? And today I made some pancakes."

"Pancakes? They'll do. Cut them into slices and put them in the bag." Not daring to look at his wife, he picked up a chopper and started to cut the piece his wife had given him. This time she said nothing and just handed him the whole basketful of pancakes. Having sliced them and put them in the bag, Longevity picked up the porridge again. He looked at it and then put it back into the pot. Wiping his mouth, he said, "Leave that for Iron Bolt."

"Eat it yourself," said his wife, finally giving in to the tears she'd been holding back.

"Don't feel so bad about it, when we win, then we'll. . . . When we have communism, then we can eat what we want, you name it." Longevity blew out the lamp and squatted in front of the grate. Dreaming about the future, he waited for Old Gan's soft knock at the door. The village dogs barked and Gan appeared. Longevity gave him the four bags, and felt bad that one held only sliced pancakes.

"Don't worry, wherever there are people we won't starve. But I'll accept your kindness just in case." He grasped Longevity's hand and then left.

When he was quite a distance, Longevity turned and started to close the gate, but suddenly found two ration bags hanging on the bolt. So Old Gan only took two. Though going off to fight, he'd left what he could for those at home. Longevity silently wiped away hot tears and shut the gate.

3. Was Longevity going against the tide or was it the other way round?

Longevity quietly wiped his tears dry with his palms and drove the cart back to the village. The other three got off as soon as they arrived and went back home. Longevity had to unharness the animals and take them to the stable on his own. Someone who'd guessed what had happened said in back of him, "Been to the County Party Committee, Longevity? Did Secretary Gan offer you some Peony cigarettes?"

"Go away!"

"Oh, you're wrong there," he mimicked Longevity, "what did Gan say, come on, tell us!"

"All right!" He tethered the horses to a trough, turned round and said in a shaking voice, "Gan offered me the best cigarettes and good green tea. He took my hand and said that as long as the Party exists, we peasants won't starve. What about that? Is that good enough?" He swung round and stormed off.

Although the pears were only as big as eggs, Longevity took a bamboo bed and went to his shed at the orchard on the pretext of guarding the fruit. He didn't know himself what was really on his mind. Anyway, apart from looking after pears he needed a few days of peace. When pears are turning sweet they attract worms and there is one kind which likes to burrow its way inside. When it gets to the core, the pear is ruined. This year, the pears looked good and the villagers had placed great hopes on them. Their winter grain and clothes for the New Year festival all depended on the pears. Imitating people who knew how to take care of fruit, Longevity wrapped each pear up with paper from used exercise books which he'd got from a primary school. Once they were wrapped, they looked even more tender and delicate. The orchard had never been treated with such honour. When passing by the villagers would shout out, "Hey, Longevity! You're making a 'Big Leap Forward' too, without making a big noise about it."

"Leap or no leap, I'm not interested, all I want to do is to stop the pears from getting eaten by worms."

During the day, he climbed up and down trees, busily wrapping up the small pears. At night, he would sit in front of his little shed gazing up at the stars. Sometimes he saw light from gas lamps dotted across the fields where people were working. Steadily puffing at his pipe, he began to realize that he was worried, even sad, and that he didn't know why. Anyway, he felt that the revolution of today wasn't like the fierce battles of the old days, and the cadres and villagers weren't as close as they used to be. It seemed nowadays that there was sort of falsehood ingrained in revolution, making revolution was like doing conjuring tricks. The yields per *mu* were twelve thousand catties, fourteen thousand catties. Now his own brigade had suddenly turned out a *mu* of sixteen thousand catties. Why perform such tricks? Who were the audience? What was even worse was that everybody knew it wasn't true but they all pretended it was. And they had the nerve to report it as good news, and send the information up to the authorities. It looked as if they were playing it up for them. What was the revolution for?

"All messed up, just turned upside down!" he murmured, still holding his long-extinguished pipe. Isn't this typical, they're not working for the interests of us peasants, they're making us spend a lot of time and energy doing conjuring tricks in order to please the higher-ups? But what about the peasants? No one cares whether they're happy or not. Longevity was immediately frightened by his own train of thought. Even his hands and feet had turned cold. Wasn't he opposing the higher-ups? Party Secretary Gan warned me to toe the Party line, am I really being disloyal to the Party?

I'd rather die than be disloyal to the Party! He leapt up, left the shed, went out of the orchard and headed for Old Han's place. He must tell him everything that was on his mind, bare his soul to the Party.

As he pushed open the door of Han's front room and put one foot inside, he was stunned to see Gan and his secretary sitting there. Gan turned to him and smiled, "Oh, just the person I wanted to see. You had some complaints about the leaders the other day. . . ."

"I . . . I. . . ." If only he had more than one tongue to say everything that was on his mind. But the more anxious he felt, the stiffer his tongue became. Flushed, he stammered and his heart pounded violently. He struggled for a moment before finally uttering, "I . . . I've just come to say that. . . ."

"Well, you don't have to say it. What you said before was very good. I've come to stay in your village to help you. The whole Party should go all out for grain production and do a thorough job and solve the problem of grain shortages. We ought to grow it wherever there's room. Grain is the treasure of all treasures, we must stress grain production first and foremost, am I right?"

"Yes, yes!" Longevity replied, glancing at Old Han who sat drawing on his pipe, his head lowered.

"Very good," Gan said firmly. "You're a veteran Party member, so I must inform you in advance. This shows the Party's concern for you. Things are developing so rapidly these days, if you can manage not to make mistakes you're making progress." Gan stopped and shot a glance at Old Han who was still looking down and puffing silently at his pipe. Longevity wasn't sure if he understood him, was sixteen thousand catties not high enough? Before he could think any further, Gan continued, but not to him, "I think you should write up a brief news item for the bulletin. Within three days, your production brigade must have a new look. We must act like lightning and not leave things undone. What do you think, Han?"

"Fine," Old Han moaned as if he was coming down with a serious illness.

"Good!" Gan said and turned to his secretary, "Write up a draft, will you?" Then he went on, "Don't shut yourself up in the office, Han. Go out and stir up the villagers. Get them to write posters to show their determination, give it a push. Longevity, you're in charge of the pear orchard, you ought to show some resolution."

"I . . . I made up my mind a long time ago, I'll do whatever the Party says." At last, Longevity took the opportunity and blurted out what he'd been harbouring for days.

"Excellent!" Gan unexpectedly stood up to shake his hand. "Then you take the lead, write a poster and paste it up on the wall and I'll have you included in the news bulletin."

Longevity was both surprised and excited, but he felt a bit puzzled. "Write what? How?"

Old Han looked up and saw Longevity's anxiety. He rose to his feet, "Let's go! I'll tell you what to write." He led Longevity outside, out of the courtyard to the village road. His sullen silence all the while made Longevity's heart beat even faster.

"What is it? Say something!"

"Listen, Longevity," said Han, looking completely exhausted. "It's been decided by the higher-ups that our pear orchard will be levelled in order to grow wheat."

"What?" Longevity stopped.

"We'll round up people and go into action tonight. Gan only allowed three days and nights, didn't he? Fell trees, plough the land, sow the seeds. That's what 'new look' means. That's what's going to be cited in the news bulletin."

"Ruined! All ruined!" Longevity's legs buckled and he slumped to the ground. He wanted to thrash about but he didn't have the strength.

"What nonsense!" Han grabbed him. "Don't forget you're a Party member!"

". . . Everyone . . . everyone's counting on the pears this year." Longevity began to wail, as though he'd been stabbed, beating his chest and stamping the ground.

"Are you crazy?" Han bellowed. "You. . . ."

But before he could go on, Longevity suddenly stopped crying and turned on him, "Speak honestly and tell me, is this right? . . . Speak up! Who are we doing this for? The Party? The old and young here in the village? Speak up! Why don't you say something? You are guilty! You're useless! I'll go and have it out with him." He turned to go but was caught by Han. "What's come over you? There's a document out about this."

"Surely they ought to know what we think before writing a document." He wrenched himself free from Han's grip with unexpected strength and headed for the courtyard where Secretary Gan was staying.

4. "Mother Earth" is not the invention of poets

Longevity went into his house but soon came out, then stepped inside again. He was in no mood to sleep. When he came out for the eighth time, the stars had begun to fade and the roosters had started crowing.

Longevity stood rooted beneath the date tree in front of his house, listening to the sputtering machine-guns and watching strings of flares in the sky. A million-strong army had gathered and had now surrounded the enemy on this vast Huaihai Plain. Good news kept pouring in. A battle on such a scale was rare. Grain carts covered long distances, creaking day and night towards the front in an endless stream. People from as far away as a thousand *li* made their contribution to the campaign, but us? Longevity's mind was in a turmoil. Wrapped in a still-new padded coat, he perspired profusely.

When roosters crowed for the second time, Gan, deputy district leader, arrived. Longevity hardly recognized him when he came in, though he'd seen him only a few days earlier. He was emaciated with sunken eyes and hollow cheeks. Circled by a black beard his parched lips were stained dark with blood. Once inside, he slumped down on a rush cushion and leaned against the brick bed.

"Longevity, quickly get all Party and Youth League members and activists together, we have to have a meeting . . . have you got some hot water, give me some to drink."

"Yes! Yes!" Longevity replied, hurrying out. He pulled two tufts of thatch from the eaves, thrust them into the stove and lit a fire. Then he poured some water into a pot and broke four eggs. While doing this, he asked, "Gan, what difficulties have you got, just tell me."

"Difficulties? Firewood! At the moment, the People's Liberation Army has got a big campaign on. We don't have to worry about grain, but the shame is that we're failing to supply enough firewood," Gan said, briskly rubbing his stubbly chin. "Local temples have been pulled down, as well as the sheds built before the land reform. What else have we got?"

What else indeed? Soon after the death of his wife, her precious little trunk had been sent to the front for firewood.

"Don't worry, we'll think of a way out." Longevity put a bowl of steaming egg soup on a low table and hurried out to get everyone together.

When he returned with a dozen people, he found Gan leaning against the brick bed fast asleep, his hands on his pistol, head on his shoulder. The soup on the table was stone cold.

They tiptoed in and silently squatted on the ground around the slumbering man. It was like a meeting between deaf-mutes; they stared at one another without making a sound. The topic was obvious: firewood. All realized the urgency of the need for firewood.

Finally, they glanced at the sleeping Gan's face and nodded at one another with determined expressions. The meeting was over.

Longevity saw them off and stood distractedly beneath the date tree. The tree was not tall but the small sweet dates it bore were delicious. During the land reform, his old lady hadn't much taken to the three-room thatched cottage they'd been given, but she was so elated over the seven date trees in front of it that she couldn't fall asleep for several nights. She gave all the fruit the first year to the army except for a very few she kept for her son, Iron Bolt, who was going to join up.

"What a splendid idea you've got!" Longevity seemed to be talking to his wife. "You had it a long time ago. They are for the soldiers."

When roosters crowed for the third time and day began to break, Longevity, having taken off his padded coat, lifted an axe. The tree was small, and with three chops it fell to the ground. The branches were already dotted with bright red dates. Early rising children all rushed over. Eyebrows arched, Longevity smiled broadly and examined the tree, estimating that it would make at most a hundred catties of firewood. That meant all seven trees would come to no more than seven hundred catties.

"Not much, but better than nothing," he thought. He began to chop another one down. When he was about to attack the fifth one, somebody caught him from behind. It was Gan. Then he saw that apart from the children, a number of adults had gathered too and were watching him in silence.

With a smile, Longevity said, "After all they come

from the earth, they can always grow again. Fell the date trees and plant pear trees. Pears are juicy and sweet, much better than dates."

Gan gripped him tightly by the arm, tears welling in his eyes, "And in future we won't need oil for lamps or oxen to plough land. Of course, we're going to have all kinds of orchards. But for the moment keep these two trees for the children."

As he spoke, the people who'd attended the silent meeting and a few others all came up, some shouldering loads of firewood, others carrying logs, large wooden chests, pomegranate trees, locust trees and the like. One old man, followed by two small children, came carrying a plank of wood.

"I haven't got any trees to fell," he said to Gan. "How about this coffin wood?"

Old Gan didn't speak. He looked round and carefully examined everything the villagers had brought him, "Villagers, you've supplied us with food and clothes. The Party will never forget your contribution to the revolution."

It was not a large village. Now, with more than two hundred trees felled, it looked rather barren. With tears in his eyes, Gan carted away a hundred thousand catties of firewood from this small place.

The following spring when a million-strong army was crossing the Yangtze River, the pear saplings Longevity had been cultivating were already as tall as a pair of chopsticks. He was overjoyed when villagers came to look at them. "Three years to grow peaches, four to grow pears. Just think, after four years I'll be damned if we fail to change them for three or four of the 'iron oxen' Old Gan mentioned." With that he sat down on the ridge by the saplings, cradled his knees, and rocked happily back and forth.

5. All you care about is pears! What about revolution?

Sitting on the ground in front of the shed, Longevity held his knees and rocked back and forth, murmuring to himself as if he'd gone crazy. Secretary Gan had just said that the revolution had now become more profound. If it weren't for his seniority, Longevity would have been swept away long ago as a stumbling block. Seeing him in such a state his fellow villagers tried to cajole him, tears in their eyes, and finally dragged him home. But he quickly staggered back and sat on the same spot again, holding his knees and rocking. He stared at the people who brought gas lamps, saws and axes to the orchard. To the sound of gongs and drums, people lifted their axes and the pear trees were felled. Branches dotted with green pears wrapped in paper lay criss-crossed on the ground. Longevity shook even more violently, and his murmuring became a cry. "Hey Gan! Come here! Where's Old Gan? I can't find you! . . ." he carefully unwrapped one pear. The egg-sized fruit had grown bigger and the green colour had begun to fade.

Heaving a long sigh, he promptly stood up and headed straight for Gan. He wanted to say, "Now, be honest, you've ordered these trees felled within a certain time. Are you doing this for the sake of revolution? To increase the autumn harvest? That's cheating! All you care about is winning favour from your superiors by giving them so-called 'good news'. You're a phoney revolutionary!" However he didn't have the nerve, nor was his tongue sharp enough. Shaking, he murmured, "Wait twenty days, just twenty days! Can't you chop them down after the pears are ripe? Wait till we've picked the pears, okay? Sow the wheat between the trees first, we won't lose any time that way!"

Worried about him Old Han, who just happened to be standing there, quickly butted in, "That's enough, Longevity! We've got to have a new look within three days. That's the Party's decision."

"Secretary Gan, can't we wait a little? Just twenty days?" Longevity was adamant.

"Definitely not!" Gan was very grave. "What we care about now is not production but revolution! We have to sacrifice our lives if necessary. Yet all you can think about is pears! And you are a Party member! Ridiculous!"

"Oh!" Longevity groaned as though physically injured. He ripped open his shirt front with both hands revealing his bony chest and said in a hoarse voice, "Then get rid of me! I've risked my life for the revolution and I'm not afraid of death. Move this stumbling block out of your way! I'm just a stone on the road, in everybody's way. I'm unable to keep up with the times. I don't know now how to make revolution. I can't understand any of it! Just get rid of me!"

"You must've drunk yourself silly!" Han tried to stop him. "Go home right away!"

Gan shook his head and sighed, "You see, this is a real test. Once he's set on the wrong path, you won't be able to pull him back."

Ultimately, the stone was moved. Longevity was dismissed from the brigade production committee and deprived of his post of orchard keeper. That was not all. At a Party branch meeting convened by Gan, he was labelled a typical Rightist who threw down the gauntlet to the Party, and was put on probationary Party membership for two years. According to Gan, "This is quite lenient because he's a veteran comrade. Otherwise. . . ." Of course, this was covered in a news bulletin indicating that the principle of "taking grain as the key link" was maintained through struggle.

Longevity suddenly aged. The lines on his face became deeper, his posture stooped. He sat all day long beneath the two date trees. People said he was dozing but he complained that he couldn't fall asleep, not even at night. He was always staring blankly with bleary, motionless eyes.

Perhaps he was staring at the pear orchard. Though wheat seeds had been sown there, the pear roots were still in the ground. Party Secretary Gan had done his job and returned to his office in the county. The brigade was praised in a bulletin. As a result of this and of Gan's special attention, they were given more chemical fertilizer, more temporary manpower from the town and more relief grain than other brigades. So what Longevity had worried about, a shortage of ration supplies, had posed no problem. The only change was that Gan was no longer the secretary of the commune Party committee — he was promoted to county Party secretary in charge of cotton, grain and oil.

Now Longevity no longer seemed to be looking for his former pear orchard. Ever since that Party branch meeting, he'd never once mentioned the orchard nor had he said a word about village affairs. He would sit motionlessly and stare off in the same direction with his bleary eyes. Occasionally his lips moved as if he were talking to someone. Sometimes he would raise his white-haired head to examine the dates on the trees to see if they had turned red or not.

And there was another change in him. In the past, children would knock the dates off the trees and eat them even before they turned red and he would say that that was exactly what he'd grown them for. But not now. He wouldn't let any of them touch a single date, not even his own beloved grandson. He picked and dried them in the sun himself and sometimes would just eat dates instead of a meal. When his son and his daughter-in-law asked him about this, he simply said in a low voice, "I'm just trying to see if they can stave off hunger," and then lapsed back into his usual stupor.

As for his bleary eyes, some said it was a symptom of mental illness, others that it was the result of irritation and frustration or that he must have been reminiscing about the past and missing Old Gan. But who knows? What was he really thinking about behind those bleary eyes?

6. All of this happened in Longevity's mind. Or did it?

The war to resist the Japanese broke out, a time of severe trials for everybody. Some of the backbones of the village militia were called up. Old Han went to meetings virtually every day, and took care to speak in high-sounding words because what he said would be printed and shown to his superiors.

It was very quiet now in the village, everyone was nervous. Although the enemy were still quite far away, their planes kept droning overhead day and night. They would circle first before dropping bombs, then clouds of dark smoke would shoot up to the sky. Those who were frightened or who'd never had any previous experience of war dashed about like blindfolded bulls. What was worse were the rumours spread by secret enemy agents. People's confidence was taking a turn for the worse.

It was just at this crucial moment that Longevity made up his mind to take the initiative in coping with the situation. As a Party member, it was something he ought to do. He had puttees tightly wound his legs, a broad leather belt round his waist with two hand-grenades on either side, an ox horn slung across his left shoulder and a long ration bag on his right. He went to the villagers and said:

"It's nothing serious, nothing at all. Old Gan's still alive and all right. He's out there just opposite that tall mountain to the west. I'm going to see him now. As long as he's there, victory is ours. All the enemy can do is try to shit on us with a few planes. What's there to be afraid of? Remember the year of the Huai-hai Campaign when the bullets were coming down like hail? My old woman was busy kneading dough and wanted some spring onions, so she walked a whole *li* to get some from her parent's backyard and then came back. She didn't take much notice of it at all. What's most important at the moment is to get organized. We need some people to dig tunnels. Our militiamen should put a sentry at the granary and send men to patrol the front and rear of the village. The ancestral hall is the highest building, so post somebody up on the roof to watch for enemy planes. If they just fly over, ignore them. If they home in on us, blow a bugle and we'll all go into the tunnel. Once they've gone, blow the bugle again and we'll get on with our work."

Longevity had become surprisingly eloquent and was moving about smartly. Having given the horn to a militiaman and slung his ration bag over his shoulder, he continued, "Next, we'll find Old Gan and get him back. I'm setting off right away. What do you think?"

The villagers all replied in chorus, "Hear, hear! That's the way! Go and find Old Gan immediately! If we have him, we'll definitely defeat the enemy whatever the difficulties."

One neighbour handed him a club made from a pear branch; another gave him a bag of finely milled wheat flour and said, "Good Old Longevity, you have to get Old Gan back!"

He said goodbye to the villagers and set off along the road leading to the mountains in the west.

And what high mountains they were! Longevity climbed them step by step without looking up. He knew that the summit was too high to be seen, but that he would ultimately reach it. Step by step, up and up. Oh these mountains, so dangerous! Menacing precipices, dark ravines, grotesque boulders, shifting soil, no path. Longevity moved carefully. He knew that as long as his steps were steady, he wouldn't fall and be killed. He crossed one ridge, but there were higher and higher ridges ahead of him. High mountains and deep valleys! Not a trace of human life. Nor any gunsmoke. Just bitter cold, heavy snow, freezing wind and icicles hanging from rocks. To find Old Gan he trudged along in the snow and waded across streams. His shoes were worn through, his clothing ripped by brambles, but he reached the summit. Looking into the distance, he saw a blurred dark expanse of land unfolding before him just like the road he had already covered. Where to look for Old Gan? Where? He stretched out his arms, and uttered a cry from deep down in his chest, "Old Gan! . . . Old Gan! . . . Come back! . . . Come back! . . ." As though helping him look for Gan, the echo ricocheted again and again through the mountains and valleys and carried far, far away. "Come back! Come back! . . ." Longevity shouted till he was hoarse and the echo seemed to grow even louder.

Flurries of snow began to fall again, covering up Longevity's footsteps. In front of him stretched a thick layer of white snow, making his journey even more difficult.

Several days later Longevity returned home completely exhausted. He had failed in his mission, he had not found Old Gan but he had learned of his whereabouts. Someone had told him that Old Gan was definitely not in the mountains but in a beautiful place where mountains were lushly forested at the top and girdled by tea plantations and orchards. At the foot, there was plenty of livestock and the granaries were full to the brim. So he was working in a place where the conditions were excellent.

Longevity decided to refill his ration bag, change his worn-out shoes for a new pair, take a short rest and then set off again. This time however, enemy planes started strafing just as he got to the edge of the village. Bullets fell about him, whipping up clouds of dust. Houses caught fire and smoke rose high in the sky. Longevity bent double and rushed back to the village. Sure enough, the granary was on fire.

Pure gold can stand a blazing fire. "We must get the grain out!" Longevity climbed over a tumbledown wall and raced towards the burning granary, but all those who'd rushed to the rescue were stunned once they got inside. It was empty, there were no sacks, no piles of grain, large or small. Only a few bags leaning against a wall. Signs on them indicated they were different kinds of grain seeds. Just as they were leaving the granary with the seed bags, the whole structure collapsed.

What soldiers fear most in a battle is not having enough grain or ammunition. Once the truth about the granary got out everyone in the village felt downhearted. It was at this point that Longevity told them where Old Gan was, and just then Han rushed in to announce that some paratroops had landed quite close by. The villagers immediately decided to go together to find Old Gan and asked Longevity to lead the way. They intended to take their mules, cattle and sheep with them and then follow Old Gan to fight the enemy. When the decision was made, they all went off home to get ready. They agreed to set off at midnight at the sound of Longevity's horn.

Longevity went home, rolled up his bedding, changed his shoes and filled his bags with dried dates. Just as he'd got everything ready, he heard three light taps on the door.

Oh! Isn't that Old Gan? That's his knock. Could he really be back? Longevity quickly unlocked the bolt and opened the door. He was shocked to see Secretary Gan instead, with unkempt hair, covered in mud and slush, clutching an empty ration bag. He was alone. Once inside he shut the door and said, still panting, "Someone tried to shoot me from behind."

"Nonsense! You're shaking our confidence!" Longevity replied sternly.

"It's true. I'll join you, I can't go all alone."

"You'd better ask the others' permission."

"Rubbish! I'm your leader!"

"And we ought to ask them about that too." Longevity had made up his mind and said exactly what he thought. He was surprised at his own courage.

"Everybody knows I'm a leader, only counter-revolutionaries would deny that. I'd just like to remind you of that without any ill feeling. Now get a move on and fill my ration bag with some food, and I'll take you into action." He thrust his bag at Longevity.

"I haven't got any grain," Longevity said resolutely.

"Humph! Look at your own bag, it's bursting, how can you say you haven't got any?" Secretary Gan sneered. "All right, if you don't want to fill it, then don't! I'm your leader, as long as you have food to eat, then I'll have my share." He fished out a slip of paper, waved it and said, "Here's the document, it's all stipulated in the document."

"Document! That won't help you get one mouthful of grain! All I've got in my bag are dried dates."

"That'll do." He opened his bag, expecting Longevity to tip the dates into it.

Just as Longevity was about to explode, there came two deafening shots of gunfire. What on earth? . . .

7. The story doesn't end here

Large firecrackers soared into the sky and exploded one after the other while strings of small ones popped continuously.

"Grandad, grandad," a small boy shook Longevity and excitedly announced, "Our production brigade has manufactured steel in a crucible furnace! Go and have a look!"

Longevity made an effort to open his bleary eyes and asked blankly, "Steal? Who's tempered steel? Where's Old Gan? Has the war ended?"

"What are you talking about, grandad? I said our brigade has produced steel! That means we can make tractors."

"Oh, tractors. . . ." That was long, long ago, Longevity remembered, Old Gan did say that one day they wouldn't need oxen to plough the land. "Tractors, wonderful," he said, "but. . . ."

He was at a loss, he'd been a farmer all his life, now they were tempering steel, manufacturing tractors. . . . His eyes closed again beneath his long silvery eyebrows. Slowly, from beneath his drooping lids, tears appeared. He was trying to remember heroic stories from his dream, but now even those had faded away. He was still a stumbling block, a stone which would have to be moved to the side of the road.

"Yes! Why not go and find Old Gan?"

He opened his eyes, wide awake all of a sudden. "I'll go and find Old Gan. I'll have it out with him. He'll surely tell me what it's all about and who in the end is standing in the way, won't he? Shakily, he pulled himself to his feet and hobbled out of the village. . . .

This story ends in January 1979. It was then that Longevity met Old Gan and they poured out their hearts to one another. What a price they had paid in search of their long-cherished ideals.

January 1979

Translated by Wang Mingjie

The Path Through the Grassland

THE desolate grassland stretched out as if to the end of the world. On a piece of uncultivated land as vast as this, one could have made straight for anywhere, but the narrow path running across it was zigzag and winding. It must have been trodden out by people who, enchanted by this scene, stared this way and that, not knowing where to go, or strolled along absent-mindedly, lost in thought. Yet, no matter how the track twisted, it was bound to lead somewhere.

Just off her night shift, Xiao Tai had got a sample from Well 48. This well was to have been sealed off because its water content was as high as 99.8 per cent. But then it had dropped to 45 per cent, and the laboratory technician had asked her to get another sample to be quite sure. With the tin in her hand Xiao Tai hurried along the winding path. Her black eyes, set rather wide apart, showed no trace of fatigue, for she was sure she would receive a letter from Shi Jun that morning. The thought of him, a young man with a crew-cut, a cynical mouth and cold eyes, made her slow down. When in his greasy overalls and boots he looked taller than in his baggy army trousers. He appeared rather lazy and sloppy, rather proud, taciturn and sarcastic. Xiao Tai had thought she had known him fairly well. But recently Shi Jun had accompanied his father south for medical treatment.

From the south Shi Jun had written Xiao Tai two letters, causing her comrades to make fun of her. Whatever for? They were the most commonplace letters which everybody could read. She stamped her feet in exasperation when teased. Yang Meng, an understanding girl, took one letter and read it aloud. That shut them up. Still someone asked mischievously, "Why didn't he write to me?"

A good question! Why did he write to her? Xiao Tai halted. On the horizon the huge sun was rising, its horizontal rays casting a rosy tint over the grassland, the path and the entire autumn scene. Collecting her thoughts, she hurried on. The fresh morning air and the sunlight filled her heart with a disturbing happiness, as if life were opening its beautiful arms to everyone.

Instead of taking the sample to the laboratory, she went to her room first. Yang Meng, small and thin, sat at the window as usual, reading a book on geology.

"Any letters?" Xiao Tai asked.

"Yes." She produced a letter from her folder and handed it to her. "From Shi Jun," she added.

Xiao Tai blushed at the mention of his name and said lamely, "I was wondering whether you'd received the admission notice from the university."

"No," Yang Meng replied in a low voice. But Xiao Tai was already too engrossed in her letter to hear her. Yang Meng went back to her reading.

Shi Jun had scribbled a sheet and a half in big characters. The other half was taken up by his signature. Another letter like the other two — one anybody could read, telling her that his father was being reinstated in his former post as Party secretary of a bureau and they would soon be returning to move house. But the last two lines made Xiao Tai's heart beat fast. "Hope to see you again. Tell me, please, how shall I introduce you to my father?"

What did he mean by that? She mulled that question over. Was this what she had been waiting for? Was it love? Then, conscious of Yang Meng's eyes on her, she said casually, "Shi Jun is coming back to move. His father is resuming his former post."

"Ah!" For some reason this news had made Yang Meng jump to her feet. Then, calming down, she picked up Xiao Tai's tin and told her. "I'll take this to the lab. You go to bed now."

Xiao Tai inquired again, "Any news from the university?"

Yang Meng shook her head and went away with the tin, her book and pen, her slight, spare figure like a flower that had withered before its time. Xiao Tai knew that some youngsters in other teams had received their admission notices already, but to mention this to her would have been cruel. Yang Meng never seemed to have any burden on her mind. She spent all her time studying the neozoic, mesozoic and paleozoic strata formed hundreds of millions of years ago. At midnight, she would get up and go to the reading-room next door, pull down the lamp and immerse herself in what interested her most. Xiao Tai respected her but had never felt sorry for her. Now that she herself had this secret happiness, she suddenly pitied Yang Meng. Running after her she said consolingly, "Don't worry, Yang Meng. You did so well in the exams, they're bound to take you. I bet you'll receive the notice tomorrow."

Yang Meng smiled and nodded appreciatively by way of answer. Then she turned away, looking worn out and listless. Was Xiao Tai extra sensitive today, or was Yang Meng really tired? Slowly Xiao Tai washed her face and looked into the mirror at a paler than usual image of herself. Her eyes preoccupied, she dimpled as if asking, "How shall I introduce you?"

The eyes in the mirror dilated and darkened and her expression grew grave as she shook her head. "No, it's not that thing called love. Love is more beautiful. He didn't mean anything special. How to introduce me, indeed! Well, my name is Xiao Tai, that's all."

She quickly undressed and went to bed, ashamed of the fancies in which she had been indulging. Making her mind a blank she closed her eyes. Although it was autumn she found her thin quilt too warm. She kicked it loose and put her arms out. Reaching under her pillow, her fingers touched Shi Jun's letter, which she pulled out and re-read. "No, he must have meant something by this question. Only he's too proud to show his feelings and wants me to take the initiative. So this is love after all?" She closed her eyes again and let her thoughts wander as she relived their encounters over the years. . . .

One night in the autumn of 1975, Xiao Tai and many other young people who had been working in the countryside arrived at the oilfield by train. Over twenty of them, who had been assigned to oil-producing teams, waited at the headquarters for their teams to pick them up. Xiao Tai and a young man called Shi Jun were assigned to Team 303. Excited at the thought of her new post and wondering who her new work-mate was, Xiao Tai looked at the young men around her. Her eyes first rested on a bespectacled youth who seemed like a southerner; but he went off in the first truck. Next she decided it must be that ruddy faced northerner who was chatting away happily. But he soon went away with another team. In the end she was left with a be-whiskered cadre wearing no socks but a pair of old gym shoes. There was no Shi Jun.

Team 303 was the farthest away. At last their truck arrived. The girl who had come to welcome her was small and sallow. Her low forehead was lined and her age was hard to tell. Only her eyes were lively with youth. She shook Xiao Tai's hand with a powerful grip and introduced herself briefly with a slight Guangdong accent. "My name is Yang Meng. I arrived here two months ago."

"Did you go to the countryside after school too?" Xiao Tai was glad to have someone to talk to.

"Yes." She hoisted Xiao Tai's heavy luggage on to her shoulder effortlessly. Xiao Tai, stumbling behind her with a holdall, saw Yang Meng with one shrug of her shoulder tip the luggage neatly into the back of the truck, just as if she were a porter.

"How long were you in the countryside?" Xiao Tai asked.

"Eight years."

"What, eight years!" She was surprised. "You must be quite a bit older than me."

"Yes. I'm quite old." Yang Meng turned to smile at her for the first time. Seeing Xiao Tai's big eyes opened wide in astonishment, she asked as she lifted the holdall into the truck, "Are you twenty?"

Xiao Tai smiled wryly, showing two rows of fine white teeth. Her left cheek dimpled and her face lit up. "I'm twenty-one. And I've been independent and seen a lot of life for three years already which makes me look older than my age."

Giving her a friendly pat, Yang Meng told her, "Let's get on the truck, another comrade is waiting for us in town."

"You mean Shi Jun?" asked Xiao Tai as she clambered in.

"Right." Yang Meng climbed up the truck. Then the driver set off.

The truck had a canvas top and two rows of seats. Yang Meng sat near the front while Xiao Tai stood behind the cabin in the cold autumn wind, not wanting to miss the night scene. "I think the father of this Shi Jun must be a VIP," she remarked.

"He was."

"Then Shi Jun's all right. His father's former boss and comrades-in-arms will look after him. Do you know him?"

"No."

Hearing this Xiao Tai went on more boldly, "According to my experience, you either avoid these people who have important connections or play up to them."

Yang Meng smiled slightly. In the darkness Xiao Tai couldn't see her; besides, she was too engrossed in looking around, but she noticed that Yang Meng paused before answering softly, "They may have had important connections before. But now, they are much worse off than other people."

"Maybe. They find things hard which are nothing to the common run of people like us: settling down in the countryside, working in the fields, cooking, washing clothes and eating corn buns."

"You're right, but you've left out the burden on their minds."

"Maybe." Leaning over the truck and looking at the clusters of lights far and near, Xiao Tai couldn't help exclaiming, "What a beautiful sight!" Turning around she said, "I like dreaming. People say I'm sentimental, but I don't agree. I think I've learned something about the world these years. As you are older I hope you'll keep an eye on me from now on and advise me from time to time. I can see that you are a good honest person, staying in the countryside for eight whole years before being transferred. You can't have had any pull. . . ." As the truck stopped a small bedding-roll and a string-bag were thrown in and a young man heaved himself in. He was of medium height, with broad shoulders and a crew-cut. He ignored the two girls and sat down at the back, but they both knew he must be Shi Jun.

His presence chilled the atmosphere. It was some time before Xiao Tai broke the silence to ask, "You live in this town?"

He grunted by way of answer.

"Is this your hometown?"

"No."

"Then how come you live here?" she persisted.

"We were sent here." He spoke caustically, implying, "That should satisfy you!" Embarrassed, Xiao Tai fell silent and was thankful for the darkness. After a while a calm voice said, "I came here because fortune smiled upon me." It was Yang Meng. Xiao Tai dimpled. Still looking out she started to hum *Song of the Oil Workers*, but stopped when no one joined in. So the truck jolted along through the grassland carrying the three young people, all equally silent but entirely different in character.

Shi Jun and Xiao Tai hadn't seen each other very distinctly that night and the few sentences they exchanged were not friendly. The following day they met again, and Xiao Tai was most embarrassed by this encounter.

In the morning she went with Yang Meng to see an exhausted well with a water content of 99.8 per cent. When they came out of the team office the bare grassland lay before her vast and desolate. The mystery and beauty created by the lights on the derricks the previous night had vanished without a trace as if by magic. Leaning against a basketball rack, Xiao Tai's eyes brimmed over. Yang Meng glanced at her but made no effort to comfort her, simply standing beside her in silence. After a while Xiao Tai wiped away her tears.

"I'm a weakling, aren't I?" she said.

"You're too sentimental, but not necessarily weak. Don't you agree with me?"

"Yes, I do. That's what I think. And I'll show you by my actions that I'm not a weakling," she announced as tears streamed down her cheeks again. And it was just then that Shi Jun walked over to accost her.

"Are you Xiao Tai?"

She raised her tearful face. "Yes, I am."

As Shi Jun eyed her intently, the cynical twist of his lips disappeared. "You don't like it here?" he asked sincerely.

"No. And I've admitted it, unlike some others." Wiping away her tears she looked him challengingly in the face.

Glancing away he said, "Let's go and get our things, the three things oil workers can't do without — canteen, flashlight and a greatcoat."

He made no attempt to hide his own dejection. Xiao Tai was at a loss. The huge red sun sailed over the horizon and a flock of wild-geese flew south in a V formation. The three young people gazed after them until they disappeared. Looking at each other again they found they were standing in a V formation too.

Yang Meng broke the silence. "Our work is underground." Taking Xiao Tai by the hand she looked at Shi Jun and said, "The oil which has stayed underground for hundreds of millions of years will escape and go into hiding when pressure is put on it. We can spend a life-time studying it. Come on now, let's go to have a look at Well 48." With Yang Meng in the lead, the three young oil workers walked in a V formation along the path through the grassland.

.

"How shall I introduce you to my father?" Lying wide-eyed on the bed Xiao Tai turned this question over in her mind. Then the sound of soft sobbing made her sit up straight. It was stifled sobbing coming from the reading-room. Who was it? Yang Meng? No. Yang Meng would never sob like that. When she listened carefully again, the sound had stopped and all was silence. She lay down and heaved a deep sigh. "How shall I introduce you to my father?"

When had that question begun to arise? It was the first Spring Festival after Xiao Tai's arrival at the oil-field when the meandering path was still covered with snow. Xiao Tai and those who had been on home leave had all returned, but Shi Jun whose home was in town was two weeks overdue. He had gone to the provincial city to visit relatives. The team leader was furious and had criticized him in meetings big and small. One afternoon, during a meeting, Shi Jun hurried in panting and sweating. He was wearing a worn-out red sweat shirt and had a padded jacket under one arm. As soon as he sat down the team leader bellowed, "Stand up, Shi Jun."

Everyone present was taken aback. Shi Jun, surprised at first, sat back more comfortably in the chair and demanded, "What is it?"

"Stand up and tell us why you are late." The team leader was still more incensed by his attitude.

"Can't you hear me if I'm seated?" Shi Jun looked squarely at the team leader. Xiao Tai clenched her sweaty hands, disapproving of the way the team leader had stormed at Shi Jun before finding out why he was late.

"You. . . . Get out of here!" The enraged team leader dashed over meaning to throw him out. Shi Jun remained seated while he wiped the sweat from his chin on one shoulder, then silently he took his padded coat and made for the door. Xiao Tai felt a deep sympathy for him, and regretted now what she had said about him that first evening before they met.

After the meeting she went to seek out Shi Jun who was standing alone in the playground, leaning against the basketball rack deep in thought. Before she got there someone took her arm. It was Yang Meng who said to her softly, "The hardest thing for a person to bear is not a dressing-down or beating, but loneliness, ostracism."

They walked up to Shi Jun. Yang Meng smiled at

him while Xiao Tai fumed, "Take no notice of a fellow like that."

"I'm used to him. What can he do but make things difficult for someone like me?" Shi Jun leaned despondently against the rack.

"It's not their fault. They have to behave that way to protect themselves," said Yang Meng, her eyes on the golden setting sun above the horizon.

"Yes. It doesn't matter if they crack down on us. They have their official posts to think about," Xiao Tai put in. Then she asked Shi Jun, "Where have you been all this time?"

"I went to the prison. Maybe you didn't know that my father has been imprisoned as a secret agent." He watched Xiao Tai's face intently with cold penetrating eyes.

She was at a loss for words.

"How is Comrade Shi Yifeng?" inquired Yang Meng. This time Shi Jun fell silent. After some time he replied, "Fine, thank you. You know my father?"

"No. I've heard about him." The setting sun turned crimson.

"You went with your mother?" Xiao Tai asked more gently.

Shi Jun shook his head, "My mother was a brave weakling. The year after my father's imprisonment, that is, the year after our family was sent here, she took a whole bottle of sleeping-pills and never woke up."

Xiao Tai gave an exclamation of dismay, but Yang Meng's face was expressionless, only her long eyelashes quivered as she lowered them to cover her burning eyes. After a while she touched Shi Jun softly on the shoulder and asked in a steady voice, "But didn't you tell us you went home every weekend to see your mother?"

"To see her ashes and my younger sister whom she left in my care. She's thirteen and studying. Children hold their lives cheap, so I have to go home to give her some warmth and faith. I want her to have faith in our father, to believe that he isn't a criminal. Mother died because she had lost faith. My sister can go hungry but she mustn't lose her courage and faith in life."

Yang Meng thought for some time and then said, "To believe in your father's innocence isn't enough. You must teach her as well as yourself not to waste your time while you're waiting, not to be soft with yourselves but to work and study hard. She's lucky to be able to go to school and to have a brother to look after her." She went abruptly, leaving Xiao Tai behind.

Her eyes filled with tears, Xiao Tai asked him. "Is there anything I can do?" Slowly, Shi Jun shook his head.

The evening rays had lost their colour. A few thin clouds hung in the sky. In the twilight everything seemed pure and calm.

The sobbing was heard again. This time, even softer, it was more nerve-racking. Xiao Tai tossed and turned in her bed. Then she sat up, but decided not to get dressed and go out to satisfy her curiosity. So she lay down again but couldn't go to sleep, though she was very tired. Gradually the sobbing stopped and silence returned. But Xiao Tai still lay in bed with wide-opened eyes.

The following Sunday, Yang Meng woke Xiao Tai up very early. When she had got up and washed her hair, Yang Meng suggested, "I've a mind to visit Shi Jun and see what I can do for him. Would you like to go too?"

"Yes, certainly. It's a marvellous idea. Why didn't it occur to me?" Xiao Tai jumped with joy. Yang Meng rubbed her soft dark hair dry, and then, putting her hands on Xiao Tai's shoulders, she told her, "The idea is good, but it just happens that I'm busy today. Can you go alone?"

"Certainly." Xiao Tai nodded in bewilderment.

Very pleased, Yang Meng pressed her nose playfully and told her, "You are like the beautiful kind-hearted girl called Snow White I read about when I was small. Now make haste and go. If any clothes need mending you can bring them back to me."

As the short northern spring had started, the wind was less biting. The path twisted through the yellow grassland. Along it drifted what seemed like a mauve flower, a flower with rosy cheeks and a flickering smile set off by woollen scarf. How would Shi Jun receive her, Xiao Tai wondered.

Shi Jun's home was at the edge of the small town. At the gate there were two stone steps, leading into a long courtyard which had at one end a well, at the other a well-tended lilac. When Xiao Tai walked in, Shi Jun was kneading dough. He was not surprised to see her, but came over to ask, "What is it?"

"Nothing," said the embarrassed girl. "I've come to see your sister."

"Oh!" More at ease, he said, "She's not in. She has gone to visit a classmate." Still standing at the door, he had shown no inclination to invite her in. Xiao Tai was disappointed at not receiving the warm and excited welcome she had expected. But now, she had to stand at the door awkwardly and tell him frankly, "I've come to see if there's anything I can do." She pushed him aside to enter the room which was partitioned into two by a sheet hanging in the middle. Virtually bare except for two wooden beds, the room was nevertheless in a state of disorder. Shi Jun followed her with a glum face. It was hard to tell whether he was pleased or annoyed.

"He's too proud." She pretended not to have noticed anything and unpicked the quilts, putting the covers in a basin beside the well. The sheets were too old to stand much scrubbing. "Yang Meng was right," she sighed. "Now they're much worse off than other people." Then she collected a large bundle of clothes and socks to be mended. Shi Jun watched her, neither preventing, helping, nor thanking her. When Xiao Tai was ready to go, he blocked the door with one arm on the frame. Fixing cold eyes on her he demanded, "Is this sympathy or pity?"

Xiao Tai had felt sorry for him. Now pity welled up in her. His pride was wounded. So she told him sincerely, "Aren't we colleagues and comrades, Shi Jun?"

"So you have come to do some good deeds." His mouth twisted cynically again.

"What's wrong with that?"

"I don't need it. I have no use for kindness and charity, don't you understand?" He was so agitated that the veins on his forehead throbbed. He seemed to be challenging Xiao Tai to fight.

But she smiled and replied, "I understand." She preferred this to gratitude. Though too worked up, he had won her respect. Smiling she told him, "Suppose I have this urge to do something? I have time. And I'm interested in doing these things. Now, aren't you satisfied?" Pushing him aside as she had when she came in, she left.

"You're lying." Shi Jun caught up with her.

"I never lie." She stopped abruptly. She had not told the truth. Turning around, her big eyes on him, she said gravely, "The truth is, it was Yang Meng's idea — I just carried it out."

Shi Jun nodded, his eyes burning as he looked back and said, "Since you have this urge, I hope you'll come again next Sunday, but on your own initiative please."

Xiao Tai had to avoid his eyes. Turning away she said, "What a lovely lilac."

"We brought it with us from the south."

"I see."

This was her first visit and Xiao Tai felt happier on her way home. Was it because she had done a good deed, or for some other reason? She couldn't tell. All she knew was that she was happy, and the grassland seemed less desolate and yellow. She returned to her quarters like a successful adventurer. In the evening Yang Meng and she looked over the bundle of clothes.

Smoothing them out, Yang Meng sighed. "His life was better than average in the past. So now when he lives the same hard life as others, it's harder for him."

"You seem to know him well, Yang Meng, and to feel for him deeply."

She hesitated before answering, "Possibly."

"But he has no use for sympathy."

"In that case he shouldn't give people reason to sympathize."

Yang Meng, a thimble on one finger, quickly and neatly mended a sleeve while Xiao Tai was still clumsily darning a sock.

Though Yang Meng helped with the mending, and though Xiao Tai and Shi Jun had no more contact than usual, word spread that they had fallen in love. Both denied the rumour, Shi Jun with a long face saying, "Don't make fun of me. I have no place for love," while Xiao Tai giggled and holding up some mended clothes declared, "Pity. These were mended by Yang Meng."

Xiao Tai didn't go to Shi Jun's home again the following Sunday as he had hoped. She went three weeks later to return the clothes. This time she found Shi Jun's home cleaner, and the fire burning merrily. Shi Jun, wearing a sweat shirt, was writing a letter. He was pleased to see Xiao Tai, and greeted her jestingly with, "Ah, the angel has come."

But Xiao Tai had not answered in the way Yang Meng had wished. She announced, "Most of these were mended by Yang Meng. So I'm not the angel." Scanning the room she asked, "Where's your sister? Gone to see a classmate again?"

"No, one of my father's fellow officers in the army came to take her away, telling me that he knew my father well and didn't believe he was a secret agent." Shi Jun laughed. It was the first time Xiao Tai had seen him laugh.

"It seems that he is the real angel of your family," said she, regretting that the clothes Yang Meng and she had sat up late to mend would not be needed by his sister any more.

"I don't believe in angels." His smile vanishing, a coldness returned to his eyes. "These last few years I have come to believe in 'conditions'. Conditions and interests determine everything. The attitude towards us of some relatives and friends changed completely when my father got into trouble. Others weren't so open about it but they put on airs, as if condescending to us. I preferred the former to the latter. This new development may be a sign that my father will be cleared pretty soon."

His words, frank and truthful, made a shiver run down Xiao Tai's back. Looking at Shi Jun and then at the pile of clothes she had brought back she said, "I hope you won't look upon this as a sign of charity. This is friendship. If you think friendship imposes conditions too, pay me twenty cents for what I've done."

"You got me wrong." He lowered his eyes and said reluctantly, "I told you that just because I believe in your disinterested friendship."

"Then you admit that in our society there exist things of value and of beauty."

"Yes. What you did made me realize that."

"Not just me. Mainly Yang Meng."

"I know," Shi Jun said impatiently, "I noticed you announced that last time. You seem to have a great respect for her. Do you know her well?"

"She hardly ever talks about herself. She's sincere and studies hard. She's concerned about you too."

"I think this scholar should be more concerned about herself. I see that most of her letters come from a farm — a labour reform camp."

"Is that so!" Now things made more sense to Xiao Tai. "That's why she understands your needs and predicament so well and has such concern for you. She must have had a similar experience."

"Not necessarily," Shi Jun said stiffly, as if insulted.

Xiao Tai remembered Yang Meng, old before her time, poring over a book at midnight under a lamp pulled down to her head, and the motherly way she mended with a thimble on her finger. She had remained optimistic and confident while befriending others unobtrusively.

"You're right," she nodded. "You're different."

"But I'm grateful to her for sending you here," said Shi Jun, eyeing her searchingly.

In some confusion Xiao Tai swung round to look out of the window at the lilac just turning green.

"That's a good lilac," she remarked at random.

"You've said that before," Shi Jun smiled. Xiao Tai's cheeks turned scarlet. He added softly, "We brought it here from the south and we'll take it back with us."

"I'm sure you will." Feeling that he was putting pressure on her which made her uncomfortable she rose to leave.

Shi Jun saw her to the door, saying, "Though my sister's gone I hope you'll go on showing concern for me, will you?"

Xiao Tai thought for a while before she answered, "Do you need it?"

"Sure." He gripped her hands.

Xiao Tai blushed again. Pulling her hands away she fled. Oppressed by the consciousness of a pair of eyes gazing after her, she quickened her steps.

Since then she had returned only once with many comrades in October 1976. Then, this summer, Shi Jun's father had been cleared of the false charges against him. Shi Jun was overjoyed when the authorities told him to take his father down south to convalesce. When he came to say goodbye to Xiao Tai he had taken the liberty of putting his arm around her waist and shouting, "We've won. Hurrah!" He then hurried off along that meandering path before Xiao Tai could figure out whether this was an expression of love or he had just forgotten himself in his jubilation.

Then he had sent her those two commonplace letters and now this one with the question, "How shall I introduce you to my father?" Xiao Tai sat up abruptly. She must seek out Yang Meng and talk to her. Just as she was putting on her clothes, Yang Meng came softly in. In her hand was a thick letter in a big envelope. Surprised to find Xiao Tai awake, she quickly stuck the envelope under her pillow and came over to sit on her bed. "Can't you sleep?" she asked, forcing a smile.

Xiao Tai shook her head, then taking her hand she inquired, "You've been crying, Yang Meng. Has the university turned you down?"

"Yes. But I was prepared for that. I'm over age. Now that they're starting to recruit research students again, next year I'll sit for that. Well 48 is back in production. Though the percentage of water is high it proves that some of my theories regarding geological analysis are correct. Once this well is back to normal I shall have a good sound basis for my theories. Then

I'll write a paper. You won't laugh at me, will you?" Yang Meng's eyes shone with excitement.

Xiao Tai was overwhelmed with admiration for the steadfast girl in front of her whose eyes were still swollen from crying. She said solemnly, "I'm sure you can do anything you've set your heart on, Yang Meng."

"No. I'll have to study English very hard for a year. Now let me tell you some good news. Shi Jun has come back with his father. He just phoned our team leader telling him that they are leaving very soon. He wants you to go to see him. Shall I congratulate you, Xiao Tai?"

Xiao Tai's reaction was unexpected. She looked at Yang Meng solemnly and asked, "Tell me what love is. Have you ever experienced it?"

Yang Meng fell silent. After a while she replied, "I've never experienced love, Xiao Tai. I've only had a proposal of marriage."

This time Xiao Tai was silent. Staring at Yang Meng unseeingly, she kept asking herself, "Is this love? Should we get married? Do I love him? And what do I see in him?"

Yang Meng's voice came to her as if from far far away. Shi Jun is leaving too, of course. The team leader said that he's going back to the province where his father's posted and may go to an oil research institute or geological institute."

"What's all that got to do with me?" mumbled Xiao Tai.

"Maybe nothing. Maybe a great deal. When will you go to see him?"

"I don't know. I might go this evening," Xiao Tai heard herself replying. Dazed she saw Yang Meng take out the big envelope and hurry off, telling her that she had something to attend to. Left by herself the question recurred to her, "How shall I introduce you to my father?"

"Let's bring this to a head and get it over with." Xiao Tai got up and, not stopping to change her clothes, set off to town. The track twisted so much that she tried to take a short cut, but she soon returned to the path, which was easier to walk on. On she trudged, her hands in her pockets, feeling emotionally enervated by the grassland's desolation, or was it that Yang Meng's strength had shown up her weakness? Anyway, she felt melancholy. Countless times she had dreamed of, longed for and waited for love. It should be as mysterious and beautiful as the moon in the water or flowers in a light mist, pure, sparkling and passionate, playing on one's heart-strings. Yet in reality at close hand it was entirely different. Xiao Tai was bewildered, not knowing which was correct — real life or her imagination.

"Everything is conditional," Shi Jun had said and he might be right.

It was late afternoon when the two stone steps came into view. Her heart beating fast, she regretted having come so early; things would have been more convenient by moonlight or lamplight. She was hesitating when she saw Yang Meng walk down the steps and hurry away. This unexpected encounter made Xiao Tai walk straight over and in. It was an entirely different room now with the luggage and chests all packed. Shi Jun was putting some things into a small suitcase.

"Was Yang Meng here?" Xiao Tai asked eagerly.

Shi Jun turned around. He had put on weight. Smiling at her he said, "I knew you would come."

Xiao Tai had to ask again, "Has Yang Meng been here?"

"Oh, yes, she came to see my father, but he had gone to a farewell dinner. I stayed behind to wait for you." He moved the suitcase off the stool so that she could sit down.

Xiao Tai saw a thick letter on the table addressed to Comrade Shi Yifeng. "Then she didn't see him?" she asked.

"Who?"

"Yang Meng didn't see your father?"

"No. It was useless anyway." Shi Jun threw up his hands in a helpless way and laughed wryly. "You see, even before my father has taken up his post people ask him for favours. Yang Meng's father worked under my father in the past. He got into trouble in 1957 and is now still working on a farm." A soft, stifled sobbing sounded in Xiao Tai's ears. As it was very hot, Shi Jun unbuttoned his shirt at the neck and sat down on a chest. "She wrote a letter saying that her father had been wronged and that he was now over sixty, and inquiring if his former unit could arrange for him to leave the farm. I can understand how she feels, but. . . ."

"But what?"

"Nothing. How can my father attend to this sort of thing as soon as he resumes office? Besides, the one who wronged her father is still in power."

Xiao Tai sat there woodenly, staring at a pile of waste paper and discarded clothes and socks which Yang Meng and she had mended. Their uselessness justified throwing them away. Still she couldn't help feeling sad. After a while she stood up to take her leave. "Your father will be late. I won't wait for him. When do you leave? I'll come to see you off."

"Three twenty tomorrow afternoon," he replied mechanically, looking perplexed, not having expected such a fleeting visit. He stood up in a flurry and only strode over when Xiao Tai was almost at the door. As his throat was too constricted to utter her name, he blocked the door with one arm as he had done at her first visit while his other hand remained in his trouser pocket. His head half turned, his teeth clenched, he still couldn't get a word out. They stood close to each other in silence. Xiao Tai was surprised to find herself so calm, even her early nervousness had gone. The little courtyard was different too, with the leafy lilac lying on the ground, its roots carefully wrapped up.

"Taking it south?" she asked quietly.

"Yes. I told you that it would be going back south, remember?" His confidence and calm returning, he asked, "Will you go back too, Xiao Tai? Have you given my question any thought?"

"You mean how to introduce me to your father? My name is Xiao Tai, your colleague and comrade, and I'm from the south too," she said playfully.

"You think that's all? This is no joke, Xiao Tai. It concerns your future."

"Maybe it does." Her voice surprised her. She was talking as calmly as in a small group meeting. "But one should work hard for one's future, shouldn't one?" She seemed to see Yang Meng's bright eyes looking at her.

Shi Jun gazed at her for a long time before saying, "You came to see and help me when I was in trouble. That's something I treasure."

Xiao Tai was touched, yet at a loss. "Shi Jun," she

said. "You want to know the truth? I don't know what to think. Sympathy, the chance of a better job and a better life — these are not love. But sometimes they seem very like it, being closely bound up together. I, well, I just don't know."

"You silly girl," he exclaimed, grasping her hands. "I didn't expect this of you. Think it over before giving me an answer. I'll be waiting."

Xiao Tai nodded and pulled away her hands saying, "I'll come to see you off tomorrow." With that she left.

The sun was setting, its afterglow giving a splendid serenity to the grassland and the path running across it. On this narrow track Xiao Tai walked slowly. A voice seemed to be saying in her heart, "How lovely to return to the south like that lilac!" This was something of which she and her mother had dreamed. It could come true if she accepted Shi Jun. That was probably what her mother had meant when she said that a girl was born twice into the world. Where did love come in then? Was she going to marry the south, a better job and, perhaps, better meals too? Love needed a full stomach, but the two were quite different things. That inner voice said again, "Don't pretend you have no feeling for Shi Jun. It may not be very deep, but it can develop. Why make it sound so bad by talking about marrying the south? Why be so strict with yourself? Shi Jun hasn't gone yet. It's not too late."

Only the small path witnessed the girl's passionate preoccupation as she walked along pondering the true meaning of friendship and love. And her wayward thoughts had their parallel in the twists and turns of the path.

Back at the team Xiao Tai wanted to console Yang Meng and confide in her all her contradictions and her decision. But Yang Meng was not in the room. At the window where she used to sit was a canvas holdall. "Has she been admitted to the university?" she wondered. But she found out from other people that Yang Meng had received a telegram saying that her father was seriously ill; she had been granted leave and gone to buy a train ticket.

Xiao Tai flopped down on her bed, totally exhausted, without even the energy to take off her shoes. She remembered that she had skipped supper but she didn't feel like eating. She just lay there as darkness closed in. Later it would make way for light again. This was like the cycle of the seasons in which life went on with each one carrying his or her own burdens, each with personal hopes and ideals, joys and sorrows. Life was pressing past Xiao Tai like flowing water, impelling her along. The easiest way was to drift with the current and let matters take their own course. Otherwise one must fight hard, especially in the beginning. But Xiao Tai was tired and presently she dozed off.

At midnight she was woken by Yang Meng. She clutched her friend's hands and sat up. "Is there anything I can do for you?" she asked. "You mustn't worry too much." But she realized that comfort was unnecessary when she saw Yang Meng's greasy overalls, hair wet with sweat and face flushed with excitement.

Keeping her voice down but unable to hide her elation Yang Meng told her, "Xiao Tai, our plan will soon succeed. Well 48 can be revived. Do you hear me, Xiao Tai?" Taking off her wet overalls she wiped her hair with them and, laughing happily, tousled Xiao Tai's

hair saying, "Just think of it, Xiao Tai. Well 48 re-
surrected! Even if it produces only fifty tons of oil a
day, that means five thousand dollars. And the paper
I've planned to write. But I'm going away tomorrow.
I'll be back within a fortnight. In the meantime you
must carry on with our experiments." She handed her
a folder.

Xiao Tai sat woodenly on the bed. Yang Meng was
like a fresh breeze clearing her mind. She had never
seen her so happy or voluble before. She had been
swimming in the current of life inconspicuous and un-
noticed, swimming slowly and steadily towards the goal
she had set herself. Her determination far surpassed
the encouragement Xiao Tai had prepared to give her.
Taking over the folder Xiao Tai nodded, unable to
utter a word. When she had dried her hair, Yang Meng
sat down beside her.

"A penny for your thoughts, Xiao Tai," she said.

"I'm a weakling after all."

"To realize one's weakness is a sign of strength, don't
you agree?" After pausing she continued, "In mechanics,
an external agent puts something still into action. It's
like a bridge leading you to the other side. But in
real life, this bridge is sometimes frighteningly narrow,
or sometimes as beautiful as a rainbow. It's entirely up
to you to choose where you want to go after crossing
this bridge. You understand me?"

Xiao Tai clutched Yang Meng's hand and nodded.
This was a parting gift from Yang Meng as well as
the declaration of her belief.

"Fine. It's time to go to your shift now."

Xiao Tai had almost forgotten that her shift was
starting. She quickly threw a padded jacket over her

shoulders, took a flashlight and hurried out. But she ran back to ask, "What time does your train leave, Yang Meng?"

"Tomorrow, no, this afternoon at three twenty."

Yang Meng had already left for the station when Xiao Tai returned from work. She had a meal, slept for a while, then changed her clothes and went to Shi Jun's home. As she mounted the two stone steps, she had a feeling that she had come too late. The room was empty except for the furniture borrowed from the oilfield. A sense of loss brought on a tender longing. "Go to the station and tell him we are closer than colleagues and comrades. . . ." As she turned in a flurry to leave, she caught sight of a pile of neatly folded clothes on which was a note which read:

> Xiao Tai,
>
> We are leaving early for the station to check in our luggage. Please return these overalls for me. Hoping to see you at the station,
>
> Shi Jun

She tenderly picked up the clothes. Then a big envelope among a pile of waste-paper attracted her attention. "That's Yang Meng's letter. They've forgotten to take it along." She picked it up, intending to take it to the station. But the letter was torn into two. She sat down on the bed. They hadn't forgotten it, only forgotten to throw it away somewhere else. Xiao Tai couldn't help putting the letter together on the table to read the lines Yang Meng had written in tears.

> Comrade Shi Yifeng,
>
> You may remember a man called Yang Shi-

chang who worked under you in 1957 when you
were the secretary of the bureau Party committee.
You know how he was punished and sent to a
farm for labour reform just because he had written
a letter making some suggestions and some criti-
cisms of the bureau's work. I was only eight at
the time. And because of that I was not able to
be a Young Pioneer and wear a red scarf. But
I sent my father the good marks I got at school
to encourage him to remould himself. Two years
later when he was no longer looked upon as a
criminal we were overjoyed. But then we learned
that once somebody had committed a "mistake"
he was a marked man for life. He had to go on
working on this farm. Seeing no future, my mother
committed suicide just as Shi Jun's mother did.
Only twelve years old I was left with a brother of
eight. . . .

Xiao Tai's hands were cold and she was shivering.
Her watch read half past two and the station was some
distance away, but she had no strength to stand up.
Wiping away her tears she read on.

Now that your family have also suffered under
false charges I believe you can understand my
anguish and difficulties at that time. Our Party
is now restoring the fine tradition of seeking truth
from the facts and today, when everybody is re-
joicing, may I also request. . . ?

As Xiao Tai rose slowly, her watch showed a quarter
to three. She must go to the station, to see Yang Meng
off and Shi Jun too. She folded up the torn letter,

picked up the overalls and abruptly left the room and its narrow courtyard.

The bell had already rung by the time Xiao Tai reached the station, and people who were seeing off their friends began getting off the train. A group of cadres gathered at the door of the soft-sleeper carriage. Shi Jun leaning half out was shaking their hands while his eyes searched around. When he saw Xiao Tai he cried, "Write to me, Xiao Tai. I'll be waiting." Then the head of a greying man appeared beside him, thin, clean and healthy. This must be Shi Jun's father. Apparently Shi Jun was telling him about Xiao Tai, for he nodded kindly and waved to her. The train lurched forward.

In the next hard-seat carriage Yang Meng sat meditatively at the window. At sight of Xiao Tai, she immediately put her rough hand on the window-pane. Tears filling her eyes, Xiao Tai waved her handkerchief vigorously as the train gathered speed.

The people dispersed and Xiao Tai walked slowly away. Then she quickened her pace, wanting to go out to the grassland into the breeze. She wanted to walk on that twisting path, to ponder what course to take through the swirling stream of life.

April 1979

Translated by Yu Fanqin

Postscript

I didn't get much chance to go to school when I was a child. My mother died when I was only three and my father left home, abandoning the five of us, who were sent to live with various relatives. I was the youngest and, along with my fourth eldest brother, went to live with my grandmother. I was already ten when I started primary school. I'd never been to school before, so I was too nervous to memorize texts no matter how hard I tried, "Once upon a time there was a farmer . . ." was about all I could get out. My first teacher is now a member of the Shanghai branch of the China Federation of Literary and Art Circles. When I first went to class and he saw I had problems he made me stay late and taught me sentence by sentence. I tried to work very conscientiously, but instead of learning the meaning of the texts, I just repeated them word by word. So I always had to stay after class and was punished.

After one year at primary school, I moved with my grandmother to Hangzhou. Not long afterwards she died. All I could do was continue studying by myself. I read whatever I could get and learned by heart passages I liked. I read *A Dream of Red Mansions* nine times, for instance, and memorized some of the poetry in it. Although a lot that kind of thing was well beyond me then, I still liked it.

I was later sent to an orphanage in Shanghai, but I

wasn't there long. In order to solve the accommodation problem, I entered a women's vocational school to try and learn how to make a living. But I still wanted to study, so a year later I changed to a missionary secondary school for girls which offered free board and lodging. I stayed there about a year and then transferred again, this time to a county secondary school. I worked hard to get my diploma. I wasn't the least bit worried about my Chinese since my foundations were fairly good, but the mathematics, physics and chemistry were quite a strain. I was a barely qualified lower secondary school graduate, with a total of only four years of schooling. But I had read an awful lot on my own, whatever I could get my hands on.

At first I read only *A Dream of Red Mansions*. In secondary school, I spent a lot of time reading Lu Yin. She didn't write much though, and the works are rather pessimistic and the plots a bit thin.

What I read the most of all were Lu Xun's short stories, I never got tired of them. I also read Soviet fiction, particularly stories written between 1941 and 1945 during the war, and also 18th and 19th century Russian classics. All of these have had rather a strong influence on me. After that I started to read lots of different kinds of fiction in translation.

I started to make a conscious effort to observe life, and to experience it and took writing as a profession in 1948. I don't usually use actual models for my characters, they're all composites. Somebody may inspire me, someone else may remind me of something, so I synthesize them into one character. In "Lilies" for example, the time, place, setting and "I" were all from real life. I myself had taken part in that coastal offensive, work-

ing at a first-aid post near the front. But the characters
and events were all fictitious.

I like short stories which have simple plot but detailed
characterization. The simpler the plot, the more the
writer can concentrate on characterization. A complex
plot takes too much of the author's attention away from
the characters. Of course, there are many successful
short stories which do have complex plots.

In the past, most of my works looked at life in a rather naive and pure light, eulogizing the beautiful. Today,
I think that was necessary. Without this kind of enthusiasm, I think it's difficult to become a real writer.
But as things advance, there are not-so-beautiful
elements left over from the old society, bad things,
things that must be criticized. You need enthusiasm
to praise beauty and criticizing what is bad requires even
greater zeal. So now another theme is gradually appearing in my work, that of castigation. But neither
praise nor criticism can be the criterion for distinguish-
ing between good works and bad. Sometimes it is hard
to draw a boundary between them. As I see it, a good
piece of writing is one in which you can see your own
or somebody else's reflection, a reflection which tells
you something you should have realized but perhaps
did not have the time to, something which touches you
to the quick. This, in any case, is the goal I am working towards myself.

茹志鹃小说选

熊猫丛书

*

《中国文学》杂志社出版

（中国北京百万庄路24号）

中国国际图书贸易总公司发行

（中国国际书店）

外文印刷厂印刷

1985年第1版